A JOUST OF KNIGHTS

(THE SORCERER'S RING)

MORGAN RICE

ISBN: 978-1-63291-131-5

Books by Morgan Rice

THE SORCERER'S RING
A QUEST OF HEROES
A MARCH OF KINGS
A FATE OF DRAGONS
A CRY OF HONOR
A VOW OF GLORY
A CHARGE OF VALOR
A RITE OF SWORDS
A GRANT OF ARMS
A SKY OF SPELLS
A SEA OF SHIELDS
A REIGN OF STEEL
A LAND OF FIRE
A RULE OF QUEENS
AN OATH OF BROTHERS
A DREAM OF MORTALS

THE SURVIVAL TRILOGY
ARENA ONE (Book #1)
ARENA TWO (Book #2)

the Vampire Journals
turned (book #1)
loved (book #2)
betrayed (book #3)
destined (book #4)
desired (book #5)
betrothed (book #6)
vowed (book #7)
found (book #8)
resurrected (book #9)
craved (book #10)
fated (book #11)

CHAPTER ONE

Thorgrin stood at the bow of the sleek ship, gripping the rail, his hair pushed back by the wind, and he stared into the horizon with a deepening sense of foreboding. Their ship, taken from the pirates, was sailing as fast as the winds could carry it, Elden, O'Connor, Matus, Reece, Indra, and Selese working the sails, Angel standing by his side, and Thor, as eager as he was, knew they could not go any faster. Yet still, he willed it to be so. After all this time, he finally felt with certainty that Guwayne lay just ahead, just past the horizon, on the Isle of Light. And with equal certainty, he sensed that Guwayne was in danger.

Thor did not understand how it could be so. After all, the last time he had left them, Guwayne had been safely on the Isle of Light, under Ragon's protection, a sorcerer as powerful as his brother. Argon was the most powerful sorcerer Thorgrin had ever known—had even protected the entire Ring—and Thor did not know how any harm could ever come to Guwayne while under Ragon's protection.

Unless there was some power out there that Thorgrin had never heard of, a power of a dark sorcerer's which could match even Ragon's. Could it be that some realm existed, some dark force, some evil sorcerer, of which he knew nothing?

But why would they target his son?

Thor thought back to the day he had fled the Isle of Light in such a hurry, under the spell of his dream, so driven to leave the place at the crack of dawn. Looking back, Thor realized he had been deceived by some dark force trying to lure him away from his son. It was only thanks to Lycoples, who still circled his ship, screeching, disappearing on the horizon and coming back again, that he had turned back for the Isle, was finally heading in the right direction. The signs, Thor realized, had been in front of his face the whole time. How had he ignored them? What dark force was leading him astray to begin with?

Thor recalled the price he'd had to pay: the demons released from hell, the dark lord's curse that each would mean a curse on his head. He knew that more curses, more trials lay before him, and he felt certain this had been one of them. What other tests, he wondered, lay before him? Would he ever get his son back?

"Don't worry," came a sweet voice.

Thor turned and looked down to see Angel tugging on his shirt.

"Everything will be okay," she added with a smile.

Thor smiled down at her and laid a hand on her head, reassured by her presence as always. He had come to love Angel as he would a daughter, the daughter he never had. He took reassurance in her presence.

"And if it's not," she added with a smile, "I'll take care of them!"

She proudly raised the small bow that O'Connor had carved for her, and showed Thor how she could pull back the arrow. Thor smiled, amused, as she raised the bow to her chest, shakily placed a small wooden arrow on it, and began to pull back the string. She released the bow, and her small wooden arrow went flying, shakily, overboard and out into the ocean.

"Did I kill a fish!?" she asked excitedly as she ran to the rail and looked over with glee.

Thor stood there, looking down into the foaming waters of the sea, and was not so sure. But he smiled all the same.

"I am sure you did," he said, reassuringly. "Perhaps even a shark."

Thor heard a distant screech, and he was suddenly on alert again. His entire body froze as he grabbed the hilt of his sword and looked out over the water, studying the horizon.

The thick gray clouds slowly cleared, and as they did, they revealed a horizon which made Thor's heart drop: in the distance, black plumes of smoke rose into the sky. As more clouds cleared, Thor could see that they arose from a distant isle—not just any isle, but an island with steep cliffs, rising right up to the sky, a broad plateau at its top. An isle he could mistake for no other.

The Isle of Light.

Thor felt a pain in his chest as he saw a sky black with evil creatures, resembling gargoyles, circling what remained of the isle, like vultures, their screeches filling the air. There was an army of them, and below them, the entire isle was up in flames. Not a corner of it was left unscathed.

"FASTER!" Thor shouted, yelling at the wind, knowing it was futile. It was the most helpless feeling of his life.

But there was nothing more he could do. He watched the flames, the smoke, the monsters departing, heard Lycoples screeching above, and he knew it was too late. Nothing could have survived. Anything left on the isle—Ragon, Guwayne, anything at all—would surely, without a doubt, be dead.

"NO!" Thorgrin screamed, cursing the heavens, the ocean spray hitting his face as it carried him, too late, to the isle of death.

CHAPTER TWO

Gwendolyn stood alone, back in the Ring, in her mother's castle, and she looked about at her surroundings and realized something was not quite right. The castle was abandoned, unfurnished, all its belongings stripped away; its windows were gone, the beautiful stained glass that had once adorned them lost, leaving nothing but cutouts in the stone, the sunset light streaming in. Dust swirled in the air, and this place felt as if it hadn't been inhabited in a thousand years.

Gwen looked out and saw the landscape of the Ring, a place she had once known and loved with all her heart, now barren, twisted, grotesque. As if nothing good were left alive in the world.

"My daughter," came a voice.

Gwendolyn turned and was shocked to find her mother standing there, looking back, her face drawn and sickly, hardly the mother she once knew and remembered. It was the mother she remembered from her deathbed, the mother who looked as if she had been aged too much for one lifetime.

Gwen felt a lump in her throat and she realized, despite all that had gone about between them, how much she missed her. She did not know if it was her she missed, or just seeing her family, something familiar, the Ring. What she would give to be home again, to be back in the familiar.

"Mother," Gwen replied, hardly believing the sight before her.

Gwen reached out for her, and as she did, she suddenly found herself somewhere else, standing on an island, at the edge of a cliff, the island charred, having just been burned to ashes. The heavy smell of smoke and sulfur hung in the air, burned her nostrils. She faced the isle, and as the waves of ashes dissipated in the wind, she looked out and saw a bassinet made of gold, charred, the only object in this landscape of embers and ash.

Gwen's heart pounded as she stepped forward, so nervous to see if her son was in there, if he was okay. A part of her was elated to reach in and hold him, to clutch him at her chest and never let him go

9

again. But another part dreaded he might not be there—or worse, that he could be dead.

Gwen rushed forward and leaned down and looked in the bassinet, and her heart dropped to see it was empty.

"GUWAYNE!" she cried out, in anguish.

Gwen heard a screech, high up in the air, matching hers, and she looked up and saw an army of black creatures, resembling gargoyles, flying away. Her heart stopped as she saw, in the talons of the last one, a baby, dangling, crying. He was being carried away into skies of gloom, hoisted by an army of darkness.

"NO!" Gwen shrieked.

Gwen woke screaming. She sat up in bed, looking everywhere for Guwayne, reaching out to save him, to clutch him to her chest.

But he was nowhere to be found.

Gwendolyn sat in bed, breathing hard, trying to figure out where she was. The dim light of dawn spread through the windows, and it took her several moments to realize where she was: the Ridge. The King's castle.

Gwen felt something on her palm and she looked down to see Krohn licking her hand, then resting his head on her lap. She stroked his head as she sat on the edge of the bed, breathing hard, slowly orienting herself, the weight of her dream upon her.

Guwayne, she thought. The dream had felt so real. It was more, she knew, than a dream—it had been a vision. Guwayne, wherever he was, was in trouble. He was being abducted by some dark force. She could feel it.

Gwendolyn stood, agitated. More than ever, she felt an urgency to find her son, to find her husband. She wanted more than anything to see and to hold him. But she knew it was not meant to be.

Wiping away tears, Gwen wrapped her silk gown about herself, quickly crossed the room, the cobblestone smooth and cold on her bare feet, and lingered by the tall arched window. She pushed back the stained glass pane, and as she did, it let in the muted light of dawn, the first sun rising, flooding the countryside in scarlet. It was breathtaking. Gwen looked out, taking in the Ridge, the immaculate capital city and the endless countryside all around it, rolling hills and lush vineyards, the most abundance she had ever seen in one place. Beyond that, the sparkling blue of the lake lit up the morning—and beyond that, the peaks of the Ridge, shaped in a perfect circle, encircled the place, shrouded in mist. It seemed like a place to which there could come no harm.

Gwen thought of Thorgrin, of Guwayne, somewhere beyond those peaks. Where were they? Would she ever see them again?

Gwen went to the cistern, splashed water on her face, and dressed herself quickly. She knew she would not find Thorgrin and Guwayne by sitting here in this room, and she felt more than ever that she needed to. If anyone could help her, perhaps it was the King. He must have some way.

Gwen recalled her conversation with him, as they had walked the peaks of the Ridge and watched Kendrick depart, recalled the secrets he had revealed to her. His dying. The Ridge dying. There was more, too, more secrets he was going to reveal—but they had gotten interrupted. His advisors had whisked him away on urgent business, and as he'd left he'd promised to reveal more—and to ask her a favor. What was the favor? she wondered. What could he possibly want of her?

The King had asked for her to meet him in his throne room when the sun broke, and Gwen now hurried to get dressed, knowing she was already late. Her dreams had left her groggy.

As she rushed across the room, Gwendolyn felt a hunger pain, the starvation from the Great Waste still taking its toll, and she glanced over at the table of delicacies laid out for her—breads, fruits, cheeses, puddings—and she quickly grabbed some, eating as she went. She grabbed more than she needed, and as she went, she reached down and fed half of what she had to Krohn, who whined by her side, snatching it from her palm, eager to catch up. She was so grateful for this food, this shelter, these lavish quarters—feeling in some ways as if she were back in King's Court, in the castle of her upbringing.

Guards snapped to attention as Gwen exited the chamber, pushing open the heavy oak door. She strode past them, down the dimly lit stone corridors of the castle, torches still burning from the night.

Gwen reached the end of the corridor and ascended a set of spiral stone stairs, Krohn on her heels, until she reached the upper floors, where she knew the King's throne room to be, already becoming familiar with this castle. She hurried down another hall, and was about to pass through an arched opening in the stone when she sensed motion out of the corner of her eye. She flinched, surprised to see a person standing in the shadows.

"Gwendolyn?" he said, his voice smooth, too polished, emerging from the shadows with a smug, small smile on his face.

Gwendolyn blinked, taken aback, and it took her moment to remember who he was. She had been introduced to so many people these last few days, it had all become quite a blur.

But this was one face she could not forget. It was, she realized, the King's son, the other twin, the one with the hair, who had spoken out against her.

"You're the King's son," she said, remembering aloud. "The third eldest."

He grinned, a sly grin which she did not like, as he took another step forward.

"The second eldest, actually," he corrected. "We are twins, but I came first."

Gwen looked him over as he took a step closer, and noticed he was immaculately dressed and shaven, his hair coiffed, smelling like perfume and oil, dressed in the finest clothes she'd seen. He wore a smug look, and he reeked of arrogance and self-importance.

"I prefer not to be thought of as the twin," he continued. "I am my own man. Mardig is my name. It is just my lot in life to be born a twin, one I could not control. The lot, one could say, of crowns," he concluded, philosophically.

Gwen did not like being in his presence, still smarting from his treatment the night before, and she felt Krohn tense up at her side, the hairs on his neck rising as he rubbed up against her leg. She felt impatient to know what he wanted.

"Do you always linger in the shadows of these corridors?" she asked.

Mardig smirked as he stepped closer, a bit too close for her.

"It is my castle, after all," he replied, territorially. "I've been known to wander about it."

"*Your* castle?" she asked. "And not your father's?"

His expression darkened.

"Everything in time," he replied cryptically, and took another step forward.

Gwendolyn found herself involuntarily taking a step back, not liking the feel of his presence, as Krohn began to snarl.

Mardig looked down at Krohn disparagingly.

"You know that animals do not sleep in our castle?" he replied.

Gwen frowned, annoyed.

"Your father had no qualms."

"My father does not enforce the rules," he replied. "I do. And the King's guard is under my command."

She frowned, frustrated.

"Is that why you've stopped me here?" she asked, annoyed. "To enforce animal control?"

He frowned back, realizing, perhaps, that he'd met his match. He stared at her, his eyes locking on hers, as if summing her up.

"There is not a woman in the Ridge who does not long for me," he said. "And yet I see no passion in your eyes."

Gwen gaped at him, horrified, as she finally realized what this was all about.

"*Passion?*" she repeated, mortified. "And why would I? I am married, and the love of my life will soon return to my side."

Mardig laughed aloud.

"Is that so?" he asked. "From what I hear, he is long dead. Or so far lost to you, he will never return."

Gwendolyn scowled, her anger mounting.

"And even if he should never return," she said, "I would never be with another. And certainly not you."

His expression darkened.

She turned to go, but he reached out and grabbed her arm. Krohn snarled.

"I don't ask for what I want here," he said. "I take it. You are in a foreign kingdom, at the mercy of a foreign host. It would best be wise for you to oblige your captors. After all, without our hospitality, you will be cast into the waste. And there are a great many unfortunate circumstances which can accidentally befall a guest—even with the most well-intentioned of hosts."

She scowled, having seen too many real threats in her life to be afraid of his petty warnings.

"Captors?" she said. "Is that what you call us? I am a free woman, in case you haven't noticed. I can leave here right now if I choose."

He laughed, an ugly sound.

"And where would you go? Back into the Waste?"

He smiled and shook his head.

"You might be technically free to go," he added. "But let me ask you: when the world is a hostile place, where does that leave you?"

Krohn snarled viciously, and Gwen could feel him ready to pounce. She shook Mardgi's hand off of her arm indignantly, and reached down and laid a hand on Krohn's head, holding him back. And then, as she glared back at Mardig, she had a sudden insight.

"Tell me something, Mardig," she said, her voice hard and cold. "Why is it you are not out there, fighting with your brothers in the desert? Why is it that you are the only one who remains behind? Is it fear that drives you?"

He smiled, but beneath his smile she could sense cowardice.

"Chivalry is for fools," he replied. "Convenient fools, that pave the way for the rest of us to have whatever we want. Dangle the term 'chivalry,' and they can be used like puppets. I myself cannot be used so easily."

She looked at him, disgusted.

"My husband and our Silver would laugh at a man like you," she said. "You wouldn't last two minutes in the Ring."

Gwen looked from him to the entrance he was blocking.

"You have two choices," she said. "You can move out of my way, or Krohn here can have the breakfast he so heartily desires. I think you are about the perfect size."

He glanced down at Krohn, and she saw his lip quiver. He stepped aside.

But she did not go just yet. Instead, she stepped up, close to him, sneering, wanting to have her point made.

"You might be in command of your little castle," she snarled darkly, "but do not forget that you speak to a Queen. A *free* Queen. I will never answer to you, never answer to anyone else as long as I live. I am through with that. And that makes me very dangerous—far more dangerous than you."

The Prince stared back, and to her surprise, he smiled.

"I like you, Queen Gwendolyn," he replied. "Much more than I thought."

Gwendolyn, heart pounding, watched him turn and walk away, slithering back into the blackness, disappearing down the corridor. As his footsteps echoed and faded away, she wondered: what dangers lurked in this court?

CHAPTER THREE

Kendrick charged across the arid desert landscape, Brandt and Atme by his side, his half-dozen Silver beside them, all that remained of the brotherhood of the Ring, riding together like old times. As they rode, venturing out deeper and deeper into the Great Waste, Kendrick felt weighed down by nostalgia and sadness; it made him remember his heyday in the Ring, surrounded by Silver, by brothers in arms, riding out into battle, alongside thousands of men. He had ridden with the finest knights the kingdom had to offer, each a greater warrior than the next, and everywhere he had ridden, trumpets had sounded and villagers had rushed out to greet him. He and his men had been welcome everywhere, and they had always stayed up late into the night, recounting stories of battle, of valor, of skirmishes with monsters that emerged from the canyon—or worse, from beyond the wild.

Kendrick blinked, dust in his eyes, snapping out of it. He was in a different time now, a different place. He looked over and saw the eight men of the Silver, and expected to see thousands more alongside them. But reality slowly sank in, as he realized the eight of them were all of what was left, and he realized how much had changed. Would those days of glory ever be restored?

Kendrick's idea of what made a warrior had shifted over the years, and these days, he found himself feeling that what made a warrior was not only skill and honor—but perseverance. The ability to go on. Life had a way of showering you with so many obstacles, calamities, tragedies, losses—and most of all, so much change; he had lost more friends than he could count, and the King he had lived his life for no longer even lived. His very homeland had disappeared. And yet still, he went on, even when he didn't know what for. He was searching for it, he knew. And it was that ability to go on, perhaps most of all, that made a warrior, that made a man stand the test of time when so many others fell away. It was what separated true warriors from fleeting ones.

"SAND WALL AHEAD!" shouted a voice.

It was a foreign voice, one that Kendrick was still getting used to, and he looked over to see Koldo, the King's eldest son, his black skin standing out amongst the group, leading the pack of soldiers from the Ridge. In the brief time Kendrick had known him, he had already come to respect Koldo, watching the way he led his men, and the way they looked up to him. He was a knight whom Kendrick was proud to ride beside.

Koldo pointed to the horizon and Kendrick looked out and saw what he was pointing to—in fact, he heard it before he saw it. It was a shrill whistling, like a windstorm, and Kendrick recalled his time in the Waste, being dragged through it semi-conscious. He recalled the raging sands, churning like a tornado that never went away, forming a solid wall and rising to the sky. It had looked impermeable, like a real wall, and it helped obscure the Ridge from the rest of the Empire.

As the whistling grew louder, Kendrick dreaded re-entering.

"SCARVES!" commanded a voice.

Kendrick saw Ludvig, the elder of the King's twins, stretching out a long, mesh white cloth and wrapping it over his face. One by one the other soldiers followed his lead and did the same.

There came riding up beside Kendrick the soldier who had introduced himself as Naten, a man Kendrick recalled taking an instant dislike to. He was rebellious of Kendrick's assigned command, and disrespectful.

Naten smirked over at Kendrick and his men as he rode closer.

"You think you lead this mission," he said, "just because the King assigned you. Yet you don't even know enough to cover your men from the Sand Wall."

Kendrick glared back at the man, seeing in his eyes that he held an unprovoked hatred for him. At first Kendrick had thought that perhaps he had just been threatened by him, an outsider—but now he could see that this was just a man who loved to hate.

"Give him the scarves!" Koldo yelled out to Naten, impatient.

After some more time passed and the wall came even closer, the sands raging, Naten finally reached down and threw the sack of scarves at Kendrick, hitting him roughly in the chest as he rode.

"Distribute these to your men," he said, "or end up cut up by the wall. It's your choice—I don't really care."

Naten rode off, veering back to his men, and Kendrick quickly distributed the scarves to his men, riding up beside each one and handing them off. Kendrick then wrapped his own scarf about his head and face, as the others from the Ridge did, wrapping it around again and again, until he felt secure yet could still breathe. He could barely see through it, the world obscured, blurry in the light.

Kendrick braced himself as they charged closer and the sounds of the swirling sands became deafening. Already fifty yard away, the air was filled with the sound of sand bouncing off armor. A moment later, he felt it.

Kendrick plunged into the Sand Wall, and it was like immersing himself in a churning ocean of sand. The noise was so loud he could barely hear the pounding of his own heart in his ears, as the sand embraced every inch of his body, fighting to get in, to tear him apart. The swirling sands were so intense, he could not even see Brandt or Atme, just a few feet beside him.

"KEEP RIDING!" Kendrick called out to his men, wondering if any of them could even hear him, reassuring himself as much as them. The horses were neighing like crazy, slowing down, acting oddly, and Kendrick looked down and saw the sand getting in their eyes. He kicked harder, praying his horse didn't stop where it was.

Kendrick kept charging and charging, thinking it would never end—and then, finally, gratefully, he emerged. He charged out the other side, his men beside him, back out into the Great Waste, open sky and emptiness waiting to greet him on the other side. The Sand Wall gradually calmed as they rode further, and as calm was restored, Kendrick noticed the men of the Ridge looking at him and his men with surprise.

"Didn't think we'd survive?" Kendrick asked Naten as he gaped back.

Naten shrugged.

"I wouldn't care either way," he said, and rode off with his men.

Kendrick exchanged a look with Brandt and Atme, as they all wondered again about these men from the Ridge. Kendrick sensed it would be a long and hard road to earn their trust. After all, he and his men were outsiders, and they had been the ones who had created this trail and caused them trouble.

"Up ahead!" Koldo yelled.

Kendrick looked up and saw there, in the desert, the trail left by him and the others of the Ring. He saw all their footsteps, now hardened in the sand, leading off to the horizon.

Koldo came to a stop where they ended, pausing, and all the others did, too, their horses breathing hard. They all looked down, studying them.

"I would have expected the desert to wash them away," Kendrick said, surprised.

Naten sneered back at him.

"This desert doesn't wash anything away. It never rains—and it remembers everything. These prints of yours would have led them right to us—and would have led to the downfall of the Ridge."

"Stop riding him," Koldo said to Naten darkly, his voice stern with authority.

They all turned to see him close by, and Kendrick felt a rush of gratitude toward him.

"Why should I?" Naten replied. "These people created this problem. I could be back, safe and sound, in the Ridge right now."

"Keep it up," Koldo said, "and I will send you home right now. You will be kicked off our mission and will explain to the King why you treated his appointed commander with disrespect."

Naten, finally humbled, looked down and rode off to the other side of the group.

Koldo looked over to Kendrick, nodding at him with respect, one commander to another.

"I apologize for my men's insubordination," he said. "As I am sure you know, a commander cannot always speak for all of his men."

Kendrick nodded back in respect, admiring Koldo more than ever.

"Is this then the trail of your people?" Koldo asked, looking down.

Kendrick nodded.

"Apparently so."

Koldo sighed, turning and following it.

"We shall follow it until it ends," he said. "Once we reach its end, we will backtrack and erase it."

Kendrick was puzzled.

"But won't we leave a trail of our own upon coming back?"

Koldo gestured, and Kendrick followed his glance to see, affixed to the back of his men's horses, several devices that looked like rakes.

"Sweepers," Ludvig explained, coming up beside Koldo. "They will erase our trail as we ride."

Koldo smiled.

"This is what has kept the Ridge invisible from our enemies for centuries."

Kendrick admired the ingenious devices, and there came a shout as the men all kicked their horses, turned and followed the trail, galloping through the desert, back into the Waste, toward a horizon of emptiness. Despite himself, Kendrick glanced back as they went, took one last look at the Sand Wall, and for some reason, was overcome by a feeling that they would never, ever, return.

CHAPTER FOUR

Erec stood at the bow of the ship, Alistair and Strom beside him, and looked out at the narrowing river with worry. Following close behind was his small fleet, all that remained of what had set out from the Southern Isles, all snaking their way up this endless river, deeper and deeper into the heart of the Empire. At some points this river had been as wide as an ocean, its banks no longer in sight, and its waters clear; but now Erec saw, on the horizon, it narrowed, closing into a chokepoint of perhaps only twenty yards wide, and its waters becoming murky.

The professional soldier within Erec was on high alert. He did not like confined spaces when leading men, and the narrowing river, he knew, would leave his fleet more susceptible to ambush. Erec glanced back over his shoulder and saw no sign of the massive Empire fleet they had escaped at sea; but that didn't mean they weren't out there, somewhere. He knew they would never give up the pursuit until they had found him.

Hands on his hips, Erec turned back and narrowed his eyes, studying the forlorn Empire lands on either side, stretching endlessly, a ground of dried sand and hard rock, lacking trees, lacking any sign of any civilization. Erec scanned the river banks and was grateful, at least, to spot no forts or Empire battalions positioned alongside the river. He wanted to sail his fleet upriver to Volusia as quickly as possible, find Gwendolyn and the others, and liberate them—and get out of here. He would sail them back across the sea to the safety of the Southern Isles, where he could protect them. He didn't want any distractions along the way.

Yet on the other hand, the ominous silence, the desolate landscape, also left him to worry: was the Empire hiding out there, waiting in ambush?

There was an even greater danger out there, Erec knew, than a pending attack by the enemy, and that was starving to death. It was a much more pressing concern. They were crossing what was essentially a desert wasteland, and all their provisions below had nearly run out. As Erec stood there, he could feel the grumbling in his belly, having rationed himself and the others to one meal a day for far too many days. He knew that if some bounty didn't appear on the landscape soon, they would have a much bigger problem on their hands. Would this river ever end? he wondered. What if they never found Volusia?

And worse: what if Gwendolyn and the others were no longer there? Or already dead?

"Another one!" Strom called out.

Erec turned to see one of his men yanking up a fishing line, a bright yellow fish at the end, flopping all over the deck. The sailor stepped on it, and Erec crowded around with the others and looked down. He shook his head in disappointment: two heads. It was another one of the poisonous fish that seemed to live in abundance in this river.

"This river is damned," his man said, hurling down the fishing rod.

Erec walked back to the rail and studied the waters with disappointment. He sensed a presence and turned to see Strom come up beside him.

"And if this river does not lead us to Volusia?" Strom asked.

Erec spotted concern in his brother's face, and he shared it.

"It will lead us somewhere," Erec replied. "And it brings us north. If not to Volusia, then we will cross land on foot and fight our way."

"Should we abandon our ships then? How shall we ever flee this place? Return to the Southern Isles?"

Erec slowly shook his head and sighed.

"We might not," he answered honestly. "No quest of honor is safe. And has that ever stopped you or I?"

Strom turned to him and smiled.

"That is what we live for," he replied.

Erec smiled back and turned to see Alistair come up on his other side, holding the rail and looking out at the river, which was narrowing as they sailed. Her eyes were glazed and had a distant look, and Erec could sense she was lost in another world. He had noticed something else had changed about her, too—he was not sure what, as if there was some secret she were holding back. He was dying to ask her, but he did not wish to pry.

A chorus of horns sounded, and Erec, startled, turned and looked back. His heart fell as he saw what loomed.

"CLOSING IN FAST!" shouted a sailor from up high on the mast, pointing frantically. "EMPIRE FLEET!"

Erec ran across the deck, back to the stern, accompanied by Strom, racing past all of his men, all of them in battle mode, grabbing their swords, preparing their bows, mentally preparing themselves.

Erec reached the stern and gripped the rail and looked out, and he saw it was true: there, at a bend in the river, just a few hundred yards away, was a row of Empire ships, sailing their black and gold sails.

"They must have found our trail," Strom said beside him.

Erec shook his head.

"They were following us the whole time," he said, realizing. "They were just waiting to show themselves."

"Waiting for what?" Strom asked.

Erec turned and looked back over his shoulder, upriver.

"That," he said.

Strom turned and studied the narrowing river.

"They waited until the river's most narrow point," Erec said. "Waited until we had to sail single file and were too deep to turn back. They've got us exactly where they want us."

Erec looked back at the fleet, and as he stood there, he felt an incredible sense of focus, as he often did when leading his men and finding himself in times of crisis. He felt another sense kick in, and as often happened in times like these, an idea occurred to him.

Erec turned to his brother.

"Man that ship beside us," he commanded. "Take up the rear of our fleet. Get every man off of it—have them board the ship beside it. Do you hear me? Empty that ship. When the ship is empty, you'll be the last to leave it."

Strom looked back, confused.

"When the ship is empty?" he echoed. "I don't understand."

"I plan to wreck it."

"To wreck it?" Strom asked, dumbfounded.

Erec nodded.

"At the most narrow point, where the river banks meet, you will turn that ship sideways and abandon it. It will create a wedge—the dam that we need. No one will be able to follow us. Now go!" Erec yelled.

Strom jumped into action, following his brother's orders, to his credit, whether he agreed with them or not. Erec sailed his ship alongside his others and Strom leapt from one rail to the other. As he landed on the other ship, he began barking orders, and the men broke into action, all of them jumping, one at a time, off their ship and onto Erec's.

Erec was concerned as he watched their ships begin to drift apart.

"Man the ropes!" Erec called out to his men. "Use the hooks—hold the ships together!"

His men followed his command, running to the side of the ship, hoisting the grappling hooks and throwing them through the air, hooking them onto the ship beside them and yanking with all their might so that the ships stopped drifting apart. It sped up the process, and dozens of men leapt from one rail to the other, all grabbing their weapons hastily as they abandoned the ship.

Strom supervised, yelling orders, making sure each man left the ship, corralling them all until there was no left on board.

Strom caught Erec's eye, as Erec watched with approval.

"And what of the ship's provisions?" Strom yelled out above the din. "And its surplus weaponry?"

Erec shook his head.

"Let it go," he called back. "Just take up our rear and destroy the ship."

Erec turned and ran to the bow, leading his fleet as they all followed him and sailed into the bottleneck.

"SINGLE FILE!"

All his ships fell in behind him as the river tapered to its narrowest point. Erec sailed through with his fleet, and as he did, he glanced back and saw the Empire fleet closing in fast, now hardly a hundred yards away. He watched hundreds of Empire troops man their bows and prepare their arrows, setting them on fire. He knew they were nearly in range; there was little time to waste.

"NOW!" Erec yelled to Strom, just as Strom's ship, the last of the fleet, entered the narrowest point.

Strom, watching and waiting, raised his sword and slashed half the ropes attaching his ship to Erec's, at the same time jumping ship over to Erec's side. He cut them just as the abandoned ship sailed into the bottleneck, and it immediately floundered, rudderless.

"TURN IT SIDEWAYS!" Erec commanded his men.

His men all reached out and grabbed the ropes that remained on one side of the ship and yanked as hard as they could, until the ship, groaning in protest, slowly turned its way sideways against the current. Finally, the current carrying it, it lodged itself firmly in the rocks, crammed between the two river banks, its wood groaning and beginning to crack.

"PULL HARDER!" Erec yelled.

They pulled and pulled and Erec hurried over and joined them, all of them groaning as they yanked with all their might. Slowly, they managed to turn the ship, holding it tight as it lodged more and more deeply into the rocks.

As the ship stopped moving, firmly lodged, finally Erec was satisfied.

"CUT THE ROPES!" he yelled, knowing it was now or never, feeling his own ship begin to falter.

Erec's men slashed the remaining ropes, disentangling his ship— and not a moment too soon.

The abandoned ship began cracking collapsing, its wreckage firmly blocking the river—and a moment later, the sky turned black as a host of flaming Empire arrows descended for Erec's fleet.

Erec had maneuvered his men out of harm's way just in time: the arrows all landed on the abandoned ship, falling twenty feet short of Erec's fleet, and they served only to set the ship aflame, creating yet another obstacle between them and the Empire. Now, the river would be impassable.

"Full sail ahead!" Erec yelled.

His fleet sailed with all they had, catching the wind, distancing themselves from their blockade, and sailing farther and farther north, harmlessly out of the way of the Empire's arrows. Another volley of arrows came, and these landed in the water, splashing and hissing all around the ship as they hit the water.

As they continued sailing, Erec stood at the bow and watched, and he looked out with satisfaction as he watched the Empire fleet come to a halt before the flaming ship. One of the Empire ships fearlessly tried to ram it—but all it got for its efforts was to catch fire; hundreds of Empire soldiers cried out, engulfed in flames, and jumped overboard—and their flaming ship created an even deeper sea of wreckage. Looking at it, Erec figured the Empire would not be able to get through for several days.

Erec felt a strong hand clasp his shoulder, and he looked over to see Strom standing beside him, smiling.

"One of your more inspired strategies," he said.

Erec smiled back.

"Well done," he replied.

Erec turned and looked back upriver, the waters snaking every which way, and he did not take comfort yet. They had won this battle—but who knew what obstacles lay ahead?

CHAPTER FIVE

Volusia, wearing her golden robes, stood high up on the dais, looking down at the hundred golden steps she had erected as an ode to herself, stretched out her arms, and reveled in the moment. As far as she could see, the capital's streets were lined with people, Empire citizens, her soldiers, all of her new worshipers, all bowing down to her, touching their heads to the ground in the breaking dawn light. They all chanted as one, a soft, persistent sound, participating in the morning service which she had created, as her ministers and commanders had instructed them to do: worship her, or face death. She knew that now they worshipped her because they had to—but soon enough, they would do so because it was all they knew.

"Volusia, Volusia, Volusia," they chanted. "Goddess of the sun and goddess of the stars. Mother of oceans and harbinger of the sun."

Volusia looked out and admired her new city. Erected everywhere were the golden statues of her, just as she'd instructed her men to build. Every corner of the capital had a statue of her, shining gold; everywhere one looked, there was no choice but to see her, to worship her.

Finally, she was satisfied. Finally, she was the Goddess she knew she was meant to be.

The chanting filled the air, as did the incense, burned at every altar to her. Men and women and children filled the streets, shoulder to shoulder, all bowing down, and she felt she deserved it. It had been a long, hard march to get here, but she had marched all the way to the capital, had managed to take it, to destroy the Empire armies that had opposed her. Now, finally, the capital was hers.

The Empire was hers.

Of course, her advisors thought otherwise, but Volusia did not care much what they thought. She was, she knew, invincible, somewhere between heaven and earth, and no power of this world could destroy her. Not only did she cower in fear—but rather, she knew this was just the beginning. She wanted more power, still. She planned to visit every horn and spike of the Empire and crush all those who opposed her, who would not accept her unilateral power. She would amass a greater and greater army, until every corner of the Empire subjugated itself to her.

Ready to start the day, Volusia slowly descended her dais, taking one golden step after the next. She reached out with her hands, and as they all rushed forward, her palms touched their palms, a throng of worshipers embracing her as their own, a living goddess amongst them. Some worshippers, weeping, fell to their faces as she went, and scores more formed a human bridge at the bottom, eager for her to walk over them. She did, stepping on the soft flesh of their backs.

Finally, she had her flock. And now it was time to go to war.

*

Volusia stood high on the ramparts surrounding the Empire capital, peering out into the desert sky with a heightened sense of destiny. She saw nothing but headless corpses, all of the men she had killed—and a sky of vultures, screeching, swooping, picking away at their flesh. Outside these walls there was a light breeze, and she could already smell the stench of rotting flesh, heavy in the wind. She smiled wide at the carnage. These men had dared oppose her—and they had paid the price.

"Should we not bury the dead, Goddess?" came a voice.

Volusia looked over to see the commander of her armed forces, Rory, a human, tall, broad-chested, with a chiseled chin and stunning good looks. She had chosen him, had elevated him above the other generals, because he was pleasing to the eyes—and even more so, because he was a brilliant commander and would win at any cost—just like her.

"No," she replied, not looking at him. "I want them to rot beneath the sun, and the animals to gorge on their flesh. I want all to know what happens to those who oppose the Goddess Volusia."

He looked out at the sight, recoiling.

"As you wish, Goddess," he replied.

Volusia scanned the horizon, and as she did, her sorcerer, Koolian, wearing a black hood and cloak, with glowing green eyes and a wart-lined face, the creature who had helped guide her own mother's assassination—and one of the few members of her inner circle whom she still trusted—stepped up beside her, scanning it too.

"You know that they are out there," he reminded. "That they come for you. I feel them coming even now."

She ignored him, looking straight ahead.

"As do I," she finally said.

"The Knights of the Seven are very powerful, Goddess," Koolian said. "They travel with an army of sorcerers—an army even you cannot fight."

"And do not forget Romulus's men," Rory added. "Reports have him close to our shores even now, returned from the Ring with his million men."

Volusia stared, and a long silence hung in the air, broken by nothing but the howling of the wind.

Finally, Rory said:

"You know we cannot hold this place. Remaining here will mean death for us all. What do you command, Goddess? Shall we flee the capital? Surrender?"

Volusia finally turned to him and smiled.

"We shall celebrate," she said.

"Celebrate?" he asked, shocked.

"Yes, we shall celebrate," she said. "Right until the very end. Reinforce our city gates, and open the grand arena. I declare a hundred days of feasts and games. We may die," she concluded with a smile, "but we shall do so with a smile."

CHAPTER SIX

Godfrey raced through the streets of Volusia, joined by Ario, Merek, Akorth, and Fulton, hurrying to make the city gate before it was too late. He was still elated by his success at sabotaging the arena, managing to poison that elephant, to find Dray and release him into the stadium just when Darius needed him most. Thanks to his help, and the Finian woman, Silis, Darius had won; he had saved his friend's life, which relieved his guilt at least a little bit for setting him up for ambush in the streets of Volusia. Of course, Godfrey's role was in the shadows, where he was best, and Darius could not have emerged the victor without his own bravery and masterful fighting. Still, Godfrey had played some small part.

But now, everything was going awry; Godfrey had expected, after the match, to be able to meet Darius at the stadium gate as he was being led out, and to free him. He had not expected that Darius would be escorted out the rear gate and ushered through the city. After he had won, the entire Empire crowd had been chanting his name, and the Empire taskmasters had become threatened by his unexpected popularity. They had created a hero, and had decided to usher him out of the city and for the capital arena as soon as possible, before they had a revolution on their hands.

Now Godfrey ran with the others, desperate to catch up, to reach Darius before he left the city gates and it was too late. The road to the capital was long, desolate, led through the Waste and was heavily guarded; once he left the city, there would be no way they could help him. He had to save him, or else all of his efforts would be for naught.

Godfrey dashed through the streets, breathing hard, and Merek and Ario helped Akorth and Fulton along, gasping for air, their large bellies leading the way.

"Don't stop!" Merek encouraged Fulton as he dragged his arm. Ario merely elbowed Akorth in the back, making him groan, prodding him on as he slowed.

Godfrey felt the sweat pouring down his neck as he ran, and he cursed himself, once again, for drinking so many pints of ale. But he thought of Darius and forced his aching legs to keep moving, turning down one street after the next, until finally, they all emerged from a long, stone archway, into the city square. As they did, there in the distance, perhaps a hundred yards away, lay the city gate, imposing, rising fifty feet high. As Godfrey looked out, his heart dropped to see its bars being opened wide.

"NO!" he called out, involuntarily.

Godfrey panicked as he watched Darius's carriage, drawn by horses, guarded by Empire soldiers, encased in iron bars—like a cage on wheels—heading through the open gates.

Godfrey ran faster, faster than he knew he could go, stumbling over himself.

"We're not going to make it," Merek said, the voice of reason, laying a hand on his arm.

But Godfrey shook it off and ran. He knew it was a hopeless cause—the carriage was too far away, too heavily guarded, too fortified—and yet he ran anyway, until he could run no longer.

He stood there, in the midst of the courtyard, Merek's firm hand holding him back, and he leaned over and heaved, hands on his knees.

"We can't let him go!" Godfrey cried out.

Ario shook his head, coming up beside him.

"He is already gone," he said. "Save yourself. We must fight another day."

"We will get him back some other way," Merek added.

"How!?" Godfrey pleaded desperately.

None of them had an answer as they all stood there and watched the iron doors slam behind Darius, like gates closing on Darius's soul.

He could see Darius's carriage through the gates, already far away, riding into the desert, putting distance between themselves and Volusia. The cloud of dust in their wake rose higher and higher, soon obscuring them from view, and Darius felt his heart break as he felt he had let down the last person he knew, and his one hope for redemption.

The silence was shattered by a wild dog's manic barking, and Godfrey looked down to see Dray emerging from a city alley, barking and snarling like mad, charging across the courtyard after his master. He, too, was desperate to save Darius, and as he reached the great iron gates, he leapt up and threw himself on them, tearing at them, fruitlessly, with his teeth.

Godfrey watched with horror as the Empire soldiers standing guard caught sight of Dray and signaled to each other. One drew his sword and approached the dog, clearly preparing to slaughter him.

Godfrey did not know what overcame him, but something inside him snapped. It was just too much for him, too much injustice for him to bear. If he could not save Darius, at least he must save his beloved dog.

Godfrey heard himself shout, felt himself running, as if he were outside of himself. With a surreal feeling, he felt himself draw his short sword and rush forward for the unsuspecting guard, and as the guard turned, he watched himself plunge it into the guard's heart.

The huge Empire soldier looked down at Godfrey with disbelief, his eyes open wide, as he stood there, frozen. Then he dropped down to the ground, dead.

Godfrey heard a cry and saw the two other Empire guards bear down on him. They raised their menacing weapons, and he knew he was no match for them. He would die here, at this gate, but at least he would die with a noble effort.

A snarl ripped through the air, and Godfrey saw, out of the corner of his eye, Dray turn and bound forward, and leap onto the guard looming over Godfrey. He sank his fangs into his throat, and pinned him down to the ground, tearing at him until the man stopped moving.

At the same time, Merek and Ario rushed forward and each used their short swords to stab the other guard at Godfrey's back, killing him together before he could finish Godfrey off.

They all stood there, in the silence, Godfrey looking at all the carnage, shocked at what he had just done, shocked that he had that sort of bravery, as Dray rushed over and licked the back of his hand.

"I didn't think you had it in you," Merek said, admiringly.

Godfrey stood there, stunned.

"I'm not even sure what I just did," he said, meaning it, the events all a blur. He had not meant to act—he just had. Did that still make him brave? he wondered.

Akorth and Fulton looked every which way, in terror, for any sign of Empire soldiers.

"We must get out of here!" Akorth yelled. "Now!"

Godfrey felt hands on him and felt himself ushered away. He turned and ran with the others, Dray at their side, all of them leaving the gate, running back to Volusia, and to God knew what the fates had in store for them.

CHAPTER SEVEN

Darius sat back against the iron bars, his wrists shackled to his ankles, a long, heavy chain between them, his body covered in wounds and bruises, and he felt like he weighed a million pounds. As he went, the carriage bouncing on the rough road, he looked out and watched the desert sky between the bars, feeling forlorn. His carriage passed through an endless, barren landscape, nothing but desolation as far as the eye could see. It looked as if the world had ended.

His carriage was shaded, but streaks of sunlight streamed through the bars, and he felt the oppressive desert heat rising up in waves, making him sweat even in the shade, adding to his discomfort.

But Darius did not care. His entire body burned and ached from his head to his toes, covered in lumps, his limbs hard to move, worn out from the endless days of fighting in the arena. Unable to sleep, he closed his eyes and tried to make the memories go away, but each time he did, he saw all of his friends dying alongside him, Desmond, Raj, Luzi and Kaz, each in terrible ways. All of them dead so that he could survive.

He was the victor, had achieved the impossible—and yet that meant little to him now. He knew death was coming; his reward, after all, was to be shipped off for the Empire capital, to become a spectacle in a greater arena, with even worse foes. The reward for it all, for all his acts of valor, was death.

Darius would rather die right now than go through it all again. But he could not even control that; he was shackled here, helpless. How much longer would this torture have to go on? Would he have to witness every last thing he loved in the world die before he could die himself?

Darius closed his eyes again, desperately trying to blot out the memories, and as he did there came to him an early childhood memory. He was playing before his grandfather's hut, in the dirt, wielding a staff. He hit a tree again and again, until finally his grandfather snatched it from him.

"Do not play with sticks," his grandfather scolded. "Do you wish to catch the Empire's attention? Do you wish for them to think of you as a warrior?"

His grandfather broke the stick over his knee, and Darius had bristled with outrage. That was more than a stick: that was his all-powerful staff, the only weapon he'd had. That staff had meant everything to him.

Yes, I want them to know me as a warrior. I want to be known as nothing else in life, Darius had thought.

But as his grandfather turned his back and stormed away, he had been too scared to say it aloud.

Darius had picked up the broken stick and held the pieces in his hands, tears rolling down his cheek. One day, he vowed, he would take revenge on all of them—his life, his village, their situation, the Empire, anything and everything he could not control.

He would crush them all. And he would be known as nothing other than a warrior.

*

Darius did not know how much time had passed when he awoke, but he noticed immediately that the bright morning sun of the desert had shifted to the dim orange sun of afternoon, heading to sunset. The air was much cooler, too, and his wounds had stiffened, making it harder for him to move, to even shift himself in the uncomfortable carriage. The horses jostled endlessly on the hard rock of the desert, the endless feeling of metal banging against his head making him feel as if it were shattering his skull. He rubbed his eyes, pulling the caked dirt from his lashes, and wondered how far this capital was. He felt as if he'd traveled already to the ends of the earth.

He blinked several times and looked out, expecting, as always to see an empty horizon, a desert of waste. Yet this time as he looked out, he was startled to see something else. He sat up straighter for the first time.

The carriage began to slow, the thundering of the horses quieted a bit, the roads became smoother, and as he studied the new landscape, Darius saw a sight he would never forget: there, rising out of the desert like some lost civilization, was a massive city wall, seeming to rise to the heavens and stretching as far as the eye could see. It was marked by huge, shining golden doors, its walls and parapets lined with Empire soldiers, and Darius knew at once that they had made it: the capital.

The sound of the road changed, a hollow, wooden sound, and Darius looked down and saw the carriage being driven over an arched drawbridge. They passed hundreds more soldiers lining the bridge, all of whom snapped to attention as they went.

A great groaning filled the sky, and Darius looked ahead and watched the golden doors, impossibly tall, open wide, as if to embrace him. He saw a glimmer beyond them, of the most magnificent city he'd ever seen, and he knew, without a doubt, that this was a place from which there would be no escape. As if to confirm his thoughts, Darius heard a distant thunder, one he recognized immediately: it was the roar of an arena, a new arena, of men out for blood, and of what would surely be his final resting place. He did not fear it; he just prayed to god that he die on his feet, a sword in his hand, in one final act of valor.

CHAPTER EIGHT

Thorgrin pulled one last time on the golden rope, hands shaking, Angel on his back, sweat pouring down his face, and he finally cleared the cliff, his knees touching down on soil, catching his breath. He turned and looked back and saw, hundreds of feet below, straight down the steep cliffs, the crashing ocean waves, their ship on the beach, looking so small, and he was amazed at how far he'd climbed. He heard groans all around him, and turned to see Reece and Selese, Elden and Indra, O'Connor and Matus all finishing the climb, all hoisting themselves up and onto the Isle of Light.

Thor knelt there, muscles exhausted, and looked up at the Isle of Light spread out before him—and his heart sank with a fresh sense of foreboding. Before he even saw the awful sight, he could smell the burning ash, the smell of smoke heavy in the air. He could also feel the heat, the smoldering fires, the damage that remained from whatever creatures had destroyed this place. The island was black, burned, destroyed, everything that had once been so idyllic about it, that had seemed so invincible, now turned to ash.

Thorgrin gained his feet and wasted no time. He began to venture out into the isle, his heart pounding as he looked everywhere for Guwayne. As he took in the state of this place, he hated to think of what he might find.

"GUWAYNE!" Thorgrin shouted as he jogged across the smoldering hills, raising both hands to his mouth.

His voice was echoed back to him against the rolling hills, as if to mock him. And then nothing but silence.

There came a lonely screech from somewhere high above, and Thor looked up to see Lycoples, still circling. Lycoples screeched again, dove low, and flew off toward the center of the isle. Thor sensed at once that she was leading him to his son.

Thor broke off into a jog, the others beside him, running through the charred wasteland, searching everywhere.

"GUWAYNE!" he shouted again. "RAGON!"

As Thor took in the devastation of the blackened landscape, he felt increasingly certain that nothing could have survived here. These rolling hills, once so lush with grass and trees, were now but a scarred landscape. Thor wondered what sort of creatures, aside from dragons, could wreak this sort of havoc—and more importantly, who controlled them, who had sent them here, and why. Why was his son so important that someone would send an army for him?

Thor looked to the horizon, hoping for a sign of them, but his heart sank as he saw nothing. Instead he saw only smoldering flames littering the hills.

He wanted to believe Guwayne had somehow survived all this. But he did not see how. If a sorcerer as powerful as Ragon could not stop whatever forces had been here, how could he possibly save his son?

For the first time since he had set out on this quest, Thor was beginning to lose all hope.

They ran and ran, ascending and descending hills, and as they crested a particularly large hill, suddenly O'Connor, leading the way, pointed excitedly.

"There!" he called out.

O'Connor pointed to the side, to the remains of an ancient tree, now charred, its branches gnarled. And as Thor looked closely, he spotted, lying beneath it, motionless, a body.

Thor felt at once that it was Ragon. And he saw no sign of Guwayne.

Thor, filled with dread, raced forward, and as he reached him, collapsed on his knees at his side, scanning everywhere for Guwayne. He hoped that perhaps he'd find Guwayne hidden in Ragon's robes, or somewhere beside him, or nearby, perhaps in the cleft of a rock.

But his heart sank as he saw he was nowhere to be found.

Thor reached down and slowly turned over Ragon, his robe charred black, praying he had not been killed—and as he turned him over, he felt a glimmer of hope to see Ragon's eyes flutter. Thor reached down and grabbed his shoulders, still hot to the touch, and he pulled back Ragon's hood and was horrified to see his face charred, disfigured from the flames.

Ragon began to gasp and cough, and Thor could see he was struggling for life. He felt devastated at the sight of him, this beautiful man who had been so kind to them, reduced to such a state for defending this isle, for defending Guwayne. Thor could not help but feel responsible.

"Ragon," Thorgrin said, his voice catching in his throat. "Forgive me."

"It is I who beg your forgiveness," Ragon said, his voice raspy, barely able to get out the words. He coughed a long time, then finally continued. "Guwayne…" he began, then trailed off.

Thor's heart was slamming his chest, not wanting to hear his next words, fearing the worst. How could he ever face Gwendolyn again?

"Tell me," Thor demanded, clutching his shoulders. "Does the boy live?"

Ragon gasped a long time, trying to catch his breath, and Thor gestured to O'Connor, who reached over and handed him a sack of water. Thor poured the water over Ragon's lips, and Ragon drank, coughing as he did.

Finally, Ragon shook his head.

"Worse," he said, his voice barely above a whisper. "Death would have been a mercy for him."

Ragon fell silent, and Thor nearly shook with anticipation, willing him to speak.

"They have taken him away," Ragon finally continued. "They snatched him from my arms. All of them, all here, just for him."

Thor's heart dropped at the thought of his precious child being snatched away by these evil creatures.

"But who?" Thor asked. "Who is behind this? Who is more powerful than you who could do this? I thought your power, like Argon's, was impenetrable by all creatures of this world."

Ragon nodded.

"All creatures of this world, yes," he said. "But these were not of this world. They were creatures not from hell, but from a place even darker: the Land of Blood."

"The Land of Blood?" Thorgrin asked, baffled. "I have been to the hells and back," Thor added. "What place can be darker?"

Ragon shook his head.

"The Land of Blood is more than a place. It is a state. An evil darker and more powerful than you ever imagine. It is the domain of the Blood Lord, and it has grown darker and more powerful over generations. There is a war between the Realms. An ancient struggle between evil and light. Each vies for control. And Guwayne, I'm afraid, is the key: whoever has him, can win, can have dominion over the world. For all time. It was what Argon never told you. What he could not tell you yet. You were not ready. It was what he was training you for: a greater war than you would ever know."

Thor gaped, trying to comprehend.

"I don't understand," he said. "They have not taken Guwayne to kill him?"

He shook his head.

"Far worse. They have taken him as their own, to raise as the demon child they need to fulfill the prophecy and destroy all that is good in the universe."

Thor reeled, his heart pounding, trying to understand it all.

"Then I shall get him back," Thor said, a cold feeling of resolve rushing through his veins, especially as he heard Lycoples high above, screeching, craving, as he, vengeance.

Ragon reached out and grabbed Thor's wrist, with a surprising amount of strength for a man about to die. He looked into Thor's eyes with an intensity that scared him.

"You cannot," he said firmly. "The Land of Blood is too powerful for any human to survive. The price to enter there is too high. Even with all your powers, mark my words: you would surely die if you go there. *All* of you would. You are not powerful yet enough yet. You need more training. You need to foster your powers first. To go now would be folly. You would not retrieve your son, and you would all be destroyed."

But Thor's heart hardened with resolve.

"I have faced the greatest darkness, the greatest powers in the world," Thorgrin said. "Including my own father. And never have I backed down from fear. I will face this dark lord, whatever his powers; I will enter this Land of Blood, whatever the cost. It is my son. I will retrieve him—or die trying."

Ragon shook his head, coughing.

"You are not ready," he said, his voice trailing off. "Not ready…. You need…power…. You need…the…ring," he said, and then erupted into a fit of coughing blood.

Thor stared back, desperate to know what he meant before he passed away.

"What ring?" Thor asked. "Our homeland?"

There came a long silence, Ragon's wheezing the only sound in the air, until finally he opened his eyes, just a sliver.

"The...sacred ring."

Thor grabbed Ragon's shoulders, willing him to respond, but suddenly, he felt Ragon's body stiffening in his hands. His eyes froze, there came an awful death gasp, and a moment later, he stopped breathing, perfectly still.

Dead.

Thor felt a wave of agony rush through him.

"NO!" Thor threw his head back and cried to the heavens. Thor was wracked with sobs as he reached out and embraced Ragon, this generous man who had given up his life to guard his son. He was overwhelmed with grief and guilt—and he slowly and steadily felt a new resolve rising up within him.

Thor looked to the heavens, and he knew what he had to do.

"LYCOPLES!" Thor shrieked, the anguished cry of a father filled with desperation, filled with fury, with nothing left to lose.

Lycoples heard his cry: she screeched, high up in the heavens, her fury matching Thor's, and she circled down lower and lower, until she landed but a few feet away.

Without hesitating, Thor ran to her, jumped on her back, and grabbed hold of her neck tight. He felt energized to be on the back of a dragon again.

"Wait!" O'Connor yelled, rushing forward with the others. "Where are you going?"

Thor looked them dead in the eye.

"To the Land of Blood," he replied, feeling more certain than he'd ever had in his life. "I will rescue my son. Whatever it takes."

"You will be destroyed," Reece said, stepping forward with concern, his voice grave.

"Then I will be destroyed with honor," Thor replied.

Thor peered upward, looked to the horizon, and he saw the trail of the gargoyles, disappearing into the sky—and he knew where he must go.

"Then you shall not go alone," Reece called out, "We shall follow your trail in our ship, and we shall meet you there."

Thorgrin nodded and squeezed Lycoples, and suddenly, Thor felt that familiar sensation as the two of them lifted up into the air.

"No, Thorgrin!" cried out an anguished voice behind him.

He knew the voice to be Angel's, and he felt a pang of guilt as he flew away from her.

But he could not look back. His son lay ahead—and death or not, he would find him—and kill them all.

CHAPTER NINE

Gwendolyn walked through the tall arched doors to the King's throne room, held open for her by several attendants, Krohn at her side, and was impressed by the sight before her. There, at the far end of the empty chamber, sat the King on his throne, alone in this vast place, the doors echoing behind her as they closed. She approached, walking down the cobblestone floors, passing shafts of sunlight as they streamed in through the rows of stained glass, lighting up the place with images of ancient knights in scenes of battle. This place was both intimidating and serene, inspiring and haunted by the ghosts of kings past. She could feel their presence hanging in the thick air, and it reminded her, in too many ways, of King's Court. She felt a sudden pang of sadness hanging in her chest, as the room made her miss her father dearly.

King MacGil sat there, ponderous, chin on his fist, clearly burdened by thought, and, Gwendolyn sensed, by the weight of rulership. He looked lonely to her, trapped in this place, as if the weight of the kingdom sat on his shoulders. She understood the feeling all too well.

"Ah, Gwendolyn," he said, lighting up at the sight of her.

She expected him to remain on his throne, but he immediately rose to his feet and hurried down the ivory steps, a warm smile on his face, humble, without the pretension of other kings, eager to come out and greet her. His humility was a welcome relief to Gwendolyn, especially after that encounter with his son, which still left her shaken, as ominous as it was. She wondered whether to tell the King; for now, at least, she thought she would hold her tongue and see what happened. She did not want to seem ungrateful, or to begin their meeting on a bad note.

"I thought of little else since our discussion yesterday," he said, as he approached and embraced her warmly. Krohn, at her side, whined and nudged the King's hand, and he looked down and smiled. "And who is this?" he asked warmly.

"Krohn," she replied, relieved he had taken a liking to him. "My leopard—or, to be more accurate, my husband's leopard. Although I suppose he's as much mine now as his."

To her relief, the King knelt down, took Krohn's head in his hands, rubbed his ears and kissed him, unafraid. Krohn responded by licking his face.

"A fine animal," he said. "A welcome change from our common stock of dog here."

Gwen looked at him, surprised at his kindness as she recalled Mardig's words.

"Then animals such as Krohn are allowed here?" she asked.

The King threw back his head back and laughed.

"Of course," he replied. "And why not. Did someone tell you otherwise?"

Gwen debated whether to tell her of her encounter, and decided to hold her tongue; she did not want to be viewed as a tattletale, and she needed to know more about these people, this family, before drawing any conclusions or hastily rushing into the middle of a family drama. It was best, she thought, to keep silent for now.

"You wished to see me, my King?" she said, instead.

Immediately, his face grew serious.

"I do," he said. "Our speech was interrupted yesterday, and there remains much we need to discuss."

He turned and gestured with his hand, beckoning for her to follow him, and they walked together, their footsteps echoing, as they crossed the vast chamber in silence. Gwen looked up and examined saw the high, tapered ceilings as they went, the coat of arms displayed along the walls, trophies, weapons, armor…. Gwen admired the order of this place, how much pride these knights took in battle. This hall reminded her of a place she might have found back in the Ring.

They crossed the chamber and when they reached the far end passed through another set of double doors, their ancient oak a foot thick and smooth from use, and they exited onto a massive balcony, adjacent to the throne room, a good fifty feet wide and just as deep, a marble baluster framing it.

She followed the King out, to the edge, and leaning her hands against the smooth marble, she looked out. Below her stretched the sprawling and immaculate city of the Ridge, all its angular slate roofs marking the skyline, all its ancient houses of different shapes, built so close to one another. This was clearly a patchwork city that had evolved over hundreds of years, cozy, intimate, well-worn from use. With its peaks and spires, it looked like a fairytale city, especially set against the backdrop of the blue waters beyond, sparkling under the sun—and beyond even that, the towering peaks of the Ridge, rising up all around it in a huge circle, like a great barrier to the world.

So tucked in, so sheltered from the outside world, Gwen could not imagine that anything bad could ever befall this place.

The King sighed.

"Hard to imagine this place is dying," he said—and she realized he had been sharing the same thoughts.

"Hard to imagine," he added, "that *I* am dying."

Gwen turned to him and saw his light-blue eyes were pained, filled with sadness. She felt a flush of concern.

"Of what malady, my lord?" she asked. "Surely, whatever it is, it is something the healers can heal?"

Slowly, he shook his head.

"I have been to every healer," he replied. "The finest in the kingdom, of course. They have no cure. It is a cancer spreading throughout me."

He sighed and looked off to the horizon, and Gwen felt overwhelmed with sadness for him. Why was it, she wondered, that the good people were often beset with tragedy—while the evil ones somehow managed to flourish?

"I hold no pity for myself," the King added. "I accept my fate. What concerns me now is not myself—but my legacy. My children. My kingdom. That is all that matters to me now. I cannot plan my own future, but at least I can plan theirs."

He turned to her.

"And that is why I have summoned you."

Gwen's heart broke for him, and she knew she would do anything she could to help him.

"As much as I am willing," she replied, "I see not how I can be of help to you. You have an entire kingdom at your disposal. What can I possibly offer that others cannot?"

He sighed.

"We share the same goals," he said. "You wish to see the Empire defeated—so do I. You wish for a future for your family, your people, a place of safety and security, far from the grips of the Empire—as do I. Of course, we have that peace here, now, in the shelter of the Ridge. But this is not a true peace. Free people can go anywhere—we cannot. We are not living free as much as we are hiding. There is an important difference."

He sighed.

"Of course, we live in an imperfect world, and this may be the best our world has to offer. But I think not."

He fell silent for a long while, and Gwen wondered where he was going with this.

"We live our lives in fear, as my father did before me," he finally continued, "fear that we will be discovered, that the Empire will find us here in the Ridge, that they will arrive here, bring war to our doorstep. And warriors should never live in fear. There is a fine line between guarding your castle and being afraid to walk out openly from it. A great warrior can fortify his gates and defend his castle—but an even greater warrior can open them wide and fearlessly face whoever knocks."

He turned to her, and she could see a kingly determination in his eyes, could feel him emanating strength—and in that moment, she understood why he was King.

"Better to die facing the enemy, boldly, than to wait safely for him to come to our gates."

Gwen was baffled.

"You wish, then," she said, "to attack the Empire?"

He stared back, and she still could not understand his expression, what was racing through his mind.

"I do," he replied. "But it is an unpopular position. It was, too, an unpopular position for my ancestors before me, which is why they never did. You see, safety and bounty has a way of softening a people, making them reluctant to give up what they have. If I launched a war, I would have many fine knights behind me—but also, many reluctant citizens. And perhaps, even, a revolution."

Gwen looked out and squinted at the peaks of the Ridge, looming on the distant horizon, with the eye of a Queen, of the professional strategist she had become.

"It seems it would be next to impossible for the Empire to attack you," she replied, "even if they did somehow find you. How could they even scale those walls? Cross that lake?"

He placed his hands on his hips and looked out and studied the horizon with her.

"We would certainly have the advantage," he replied. "We could kill a hundred of theirs for every one of ours. But the problem is, they have millions to spare—we have thousands. Eventually, they will win."

"Would they sacrifice millions for a small corner of the Empire?" she asked, knowing the answer before she even asked it. After all, she had witnessed firsthand what they had given up to attack the Ring.

"They are ruthless for conquest," he said. "They would sacrifice anything. That is their way. They would never give up. That is what I know."

"Then how can I help, my liege?" she asked.

He sighed, quiet for a long time, looking out at the skyline.

"I need you to help me save the Ridge," he said finally, looking her, an intense gravity in his eyes.

"But how?" she asked, confused.

"Our prophecies speak of the arrival of an outsider," he said. "A woman. From another kingdom, across the sea. They speak of her saving the Ridge, of her leading our people across the desert. I never knew of what they meant, until this day. I believe that woman is you."

Gwen felt a chill at his words; her heart was still aching from her people's exile, from the ruin of the Ring, aching for Thor and Guwayne. She could not stand the idea of being burdened with another leadership.

"The Ridge is dying," he continued, as she stood there silently. "Each day, our shores, our water source, are drying up. By the time my children's lifetime is over, the waters will be replaced by drought, and our food source will be gone. I must think to the future, as my fathers refused to do. Taking action is no longer an option—it is a necessity."

"But what action?" she asked.

He sighed, staring out at the horizon.

"There is a way to save the Ridge," he said. "It is rumored to be written of the ancient books, the ones guarded by the Light Seekers."

She stared back, puzzled.

"Light Seekers?" she asked.

"You see, my kingdom, too, is infected with a cancer," he explained. "As perfect as all looks from walking our streets, all here is far from perfect. A vine grows amongst my people, and it is the vine of a belief. A religion. A cult. The Light Seekers. It adds followers by the day, and it has spread to every corner of my capital. It has reached even to the heart of my very own family. Can you imagine? A King's own family?"

She tried to process it all, but could not follow his story.

"Eldof. He is their leader, a human, just like us, who believes himself a god. He preaches his false religion to all of his false prophets, and they will do anything he says. Many of my people are now more likely to obey his commands than mine."

He stared at her, concern etched across his too-lined face.

"I am in a dangerous position here," he added. "We all are. And not just from what lies beyond the Ridge."

So many questions raced through Gwen's mind, but she did not want to pry; instead, she gave him time to think it all through and to ask of her what he wanted.

"The ancient books are rumored to exist deep within his monastery," he finally added, after a long silence in which he rubbed his beard, staring at the floor as if lost in memory. "I have ransacked it many times—but to no avail. Of course, they may not exist at all—but I believe they do. And I believe they hold the answer."

He turned to her.

"I need you to enter the monastery," he said. "Befriend Eldof. Find the books. Find me the secret I need to save my people."

Gwen struggled to understand, her mind reeling from all the information.

"So you want me to meet Eldof?" she asked. "The cult leader?"

"Not him," the King replied. "But his head priest. My son. Kristof."

Gwen stared at him, shocked.

"Your *son*?" she asked.

The King nodded back, his eyes moist.

"I am ashamed to admit," he replied. "My son is all but lost to me. But perhaps he shall listen to you, an outsider. I implore. It is a father's wish. And it is for the sake of the Ridge."

As overwhelmed as she was, feeling as if she had just been thrust into the middle of a political and family drama, Gwen still felt infused with a sense of mission.

"I will do whatever I can to help you," she said, meaning it.

A look of relief crossed his face.

"Is that all you wish from me?" she asked. "It seems a simple task."

He shook his head.

"If the prophecies speak truly," he said, his voice grave, "then we will fail. The Ridge will fail. All that you see here before you will be destroyed."

She felt a chill at his words, and felt them to be true as he uttered them.

"The destruction is coming sooner than we may think. And then, I will need you most. When I die, my people will be a shepherd without a flock. Of course, my sons will inherit and they will rule well. But the prophecies speak of even them dying. And if they do not survive, if we are ruler-less, I will need you to lead my people away from here. To safety."

Gwen shook her head slowly, sadly.

"You speak of tragic prophecies," she said. "Prophecies which I pray shall never come to pass."

"Vow to me," he said, grasping her wrist, his eyes aglow with intensity. "Vow to me that you will save my people."

She stared back for a long time, listening to the howling of the desert winds, then finally, she knew she could not refuse the pleadings of a desperate, dying father.

She nodded back, and as she did, she felt with certainty that her life was about to change dramatically.

CHAPTER TEN

Kendrick galloped out in front of his half-dozen Silver, Brandt and Atme beside him, while beside them charged the knights of the Ridge, led by Koldo, all riding together, as they had been all day, deeper and deeper into the limitless waste. Kendrick looked down as they went, watching the trail that he and Gwendolyn and the others had left, amazed it stretched as far as it did. He had never imagined that they had actually trekked that far; he did not see how it was physically possible beneath these suns. The thought of it was staggering. Even on horseback, charging at full speed, it was taking nearly the entire day. It made him realize what the human body and mind could do when pressed to their limits.

Each time Kendrick glanced down and expected the trail to finally end, it kept going. He was beginning to feel a deepening sense of foreboding in his stomach; being back out here was bringing back bad memories, still fresh, ones he did not wish to relive. He just wanted this trail to end already, to turn back with the sweepers and begin heading back to the Ridge.

Kendrick did not like the way things were going: he trusted some of these Ridge men, and respected the King's sons, but others he was uncertain of—and some he outright loathed, such as Naten. He wondered if they would have his back if it came down to it. There was nothing worse than heading into battle unsure of the loyalty of the men at your side.

"Up ahead!" shouted a voice.

Kendrick peered down, wiping sweat from his brow, and still saw the trail, and was unsure what the others were speaking of. But then he saw the other men looking not down but up, and as he did, he saw it: there, on the horizon, stood a twisted black tree, its branches so thick with thorns that one could not see through them. As he saw it he had a flashback: he recalled him and Gwendolyn and the others all collapsing beneath that tree, beneath its flimsy shade, resting there for he did not know how long, until somehow they finally managed the strength to go on again. He recalled a brutal sandstorm had swept through while they were lying there, and their spending the night riding it out. He remembered waking the next morning, looking behind him, and being amazed to see that the sandstorm had erased their entire trail behind them, as if they had never existed.

They had all woken too tired to go on, and yet somehow, they did. He knew that if they had not gotten up from beneath it, all of them would have died there.

The horses now slowed, coming to a stop beneath the tree, and they all dismounted, breathing hard, covered in dust, giving their horses drink. It felt good to stand and stretch his legs, and he leaned back and drank long and hard from his sack, the water now warm, but refreshing nonetheless.

Kendrick stood there beside Brandt and Atme and looked up the tree, its branches made of long thorns, all twisted from too many desert storms. Kendrick looked out, past the tree, at the smooth sands of the desert beyond and saw that they were pristine. Untraceable.

Their trail ended here.

Koldo came up beside Kendrick and motioned to him at the sands beyond, examining them.

"It appears your trail ends here," he said to Kendrick, puzzled.

Kendrick nodded.

"A storm swept through here," he replied.

"You are lucky to have lived," Ludvig chimed in.

Koldo nodded, satisfied.

"Very good," he said. "Then this is where we shall begin our sweep—from here back to the Ridge."

"And what if he is wrong?" came a voice.

Kendrick turned to see Naten staring back at him angrily.

"What if their trail picks up again, out there somewhere?" Naten added.

Koldo frowned.

"Of course the trail picks up somewhere," Koldo replied, curt. "But what matters is that it does not lead all the way to this spot. There is a break in it, and that is what matters. From this spot, as far as I can see, there is nothing. Do you see something I do not?"

Naten frowned, turned, and walked away, clearly unable to respond.

"Prepare your sweepers!" Koldo commanded firmly, then turned and headed back to his horse.

His men broke into action, each extracting from their saddles long sweepers, poles with a smooth, rake-like attachment at one end, wide and flat, and attached them to the back of their horses. They were flexible, sweeping in different directions, so as not to give a uniform look to any sweeping they did, and completely erasing any possible trail. Kendrick admired them: they were clearly ingenious devices.

"We still have time to return to the Ridge before dark falls," Koldo said, turning and looking back with hope toward the Ridge.

"There better be," Naten said, coming up beside Kendrick. "If we don't, we're going to spend a long night out in this desert—and it's all going to be your fault."

Kendrick scowled, fed up.

"What is your problem with me?" he demanded.

Naten scowled back, confronting him.

"Our lives were perfect," he said. "Before you showed up."

"I haven't ruined your precious Ridge," Kendrick snapped.

"It seems like you've ruined every place you've come from," Naten countered.

"You lack respect," Kendrick replied. "And hospitality. Two sacred virtues. As much as I dislike you, I would have welcomed you into my homeland, a stranger. I would have even fought for you."

Naten scoffed.

"Then we are very different people," he replied. "I would not fight for you—and if I had my choice, I would never let you into our—"

Suddenly, a shriek cut through the air, interrupting them, raising the hair on the back of Kendrick's spine.

And then, complete chaos.

Before Kendrick could grasp what was happening, he heard a man cry out in pain, an awful shriek, and out of the corner of his eye, he saw something dark and hairy drop down from the sky and land on his throat.

Kendrick turned as he sensed motion from up above.

"TREE CLINGERS!" a man shouted.

Kendrick looked up and was horrified to see that the thick branches of the tree were filled with glowing yellow eyes. A group of small monsters, with black fur and long claws and fangs, looking like sloths, began to reveal themselves, jumping out of the branches and leaping onto the men. Their claws shined in the air, several feet long, as sharp as swords, and they raised them high and swung them down like machetes, jumping right for the group of men.

Kendrick reached to draw his sword, but it was too late. Before he could react, a tree clinger, its long claws extended, swung right for his face—and there was nothing he could do to stop it.

CHAPTER ELEVEN

Boku hung on the crucifix that the Empire soldiers had nailed him to days ago, the last of his people alive since the great slaughter, somehow, despite his wishes, still clinging to life. He had stopped feeling the pain and agony—that had passed days ago. He no longer felt the agony searing through his palms, no longer felt the dehydration, the burning of the suns on his skin. He was beyond all that now, so close to death. All that he still felt was his intense grief for his people, all of whom had died beside him in their siege of Volusia, all massacred before his eyes. He craved to see them all again, and had cursed the gods that he had been left alive.

But Boku was too spent to even have room to curse now. There was nothing left in him but to die. He prayed to the gods with all he was to please let him die—and yet for some reason, they kept denying him. For days, the Empire had inflicted on him every kind of torture before finally nailing him to the cross, and still, no matter how much he craved it, he would not die. He drifted now in and out of consciousness, seeing his forefathers in a cloud of light, expecting any moment to be embraced by them, and wishing it to be so.

Boku opened his eyes—he did not know how much time had passed—and found himself to still be alive, caught in his harsh reality, his body numb, no longer feeling his hands or legs, and having to look down and see the piles of corpses of all the people he once knew and loved. When, he wondered, would this hell end? He would give anything for a swift, merciful death.

"Bring him down," called out the voice of an Empire taskmaster, and for a moment, Boku's heart leapt as he wondered if his prayers had been answered.

Boku felt his world shift, felt his cross lowered, felt his body go flat, then borne on the shoulders of several soldiers. He was set down on the ground with a bang, as they dropped him the last few feet, and a sharp pain shot up his spine, surprising him. He did not think he had any room left for pain.

Boku looked up, squinted into the glaring sun, until suddenly, a shadow passed over his face, and he opened his eyes wide to see the cruel Empire taskmaster, scowling down at him with his long fangs and horns. The taskmaster reached over with a pitcher and dumped freezing water on his face.

Boku felt like he was drowning. He felt the water go up his nose, felt himself immersed in it, and gasped as all the Empire soldiers laughed cruelly around him.

Boku felt water on his lips, and he licked them, trying to drink, desperate to be able to swallow. But there was none left to drink, adding cruelty to the torture.

Boku blinked and looked up at the taskmaster's face, wondering again what he could possibly want, why he would bother keeping him alive. Why would he give him water? To prolong his torture, surely.

"Where are your friends?" he demanded, leaning over, his bad breath filling Boku's face.

Boku blinked, confused.

"What friends?" he tried to ask, but his throat was too parched for the words to come out.

"Those from across the sea," the man demanded. "Those of the white race. The ones you harbored in your village. The ones who fled. Where did they go?"

Boku blinked, his head splitting, trying to understand, his mind working slowly after so many days of silence and agony. Slowly, it came back to him. Before the massacre, that woman, what was her name....Gwendolyn. Yes. Her people....

It all slowly came back to him: they had fled before the battle. They had trekked out to the Great Waste, to try to find the Second Ring...backup for their army. Most likely, the Waste had taken them, too.

Boku looked up at the scowling face of the taskmaster, and realized now what he wanted, why he had kept him alive, had tortured him. It wasn't enough for them to have killed him and all his people. They wanted to kill Gwendolyn and her people, too.

Boku felt a fresh resolve within him. If he had been unable to save his people, at least he could now save Gwendolyn.

Boku managed to clear his throat enough to speak:

"She went back across the sea," he lied firmly.

The taskmaster grinned down, took a long, sharp dagger-like weapon with a curved tip, and plunged it into Boku's ribs.

Boku shrieked screamed as he crammed it in farther, turning and twisting it; he felt as if his insides were being destroyed.

"You are not a very good liar," the taskmaster said. "We found their ships burned. How could she have crossed the sea?"

Boku shrieked, blood coming from his mouth, determined not to speak.

"I will ask you but one more time," he demanded. "Where did she go? Where are they hiding? Her people are not among the dead, and we have already ransacked your village—and all your caves. They are nowhere to be found. Tell me where they are, and I will kill you quickly."

Boku's pain was unimaginable, but he gritted his teeth and shook his head, tears coming from his eyes, determined not to give Gwendolyn up. With one great burst of energy, he managed to spit. He watched in satisfaction as blood from his mouth sprayed into the Empire taskmaster's eyes.

The taskmaster, furious, reached down with both hands, pulled out the corkscrew, and plunged it into Boku's chest. Boku felt an even worse agony, as the man pushed down with all his might, turning and twisting. He felt his bones breaking in every direction, an agony even he could not bear. He would do anything to make it stop. Anything in the world.

"I beg you!" Boku pleaded.

"Tell me!" the taskmaster replied.

"The…Waste," Boku found himself screaming, involuntarily. "The Great Waste. I swear to you! I swear it!"

Boku wept, ashamed he had given them up. He had wanted more than anything to protect them, but the pain had been too intense, taking over his brain, making him unable to think straight.

Finally, the Empire soldier stopped, satisfied, and grinned down at him.

"I actually believe you," he said. "Though I am sorry to say—it won't save you."

Several Empire soldiers stepped forward, daggers drawn—and Boku felt himself pierced by a million knives, in pain from every corner of his body.

Finally, he was able to let go. Finally, sweet death came for him.

Before leaving it all, embracing his ancestors, the great light, one final thought came to him:

I am sorry, Gwendolyn. I betrayed you. I betrayed you.

CHAPTER TWELVE

Erec stood at the stern of his ship, taking up the rear of his fleet as they all continued to sail upriver, and he looked out behind them, downriver, watching the twisting river for any sign of the Empire. On the horizon, he could still see the faint outline of black smoke from where they had created a blockade and had set the ships on fire, and judging by the smoke, it was still burning strongly. Given how tightly wedged those ships were in such a narrow area—and given the fires keeping them at bay—Erec felt confident that the Empire could not break through quickly. Erec imagined they might have to resort to ropes and grappling hooks to pull away the debris. It would be a slow and tedious process. It had bought Erec and his fleet the precious lead they needed.

Erec turned and looked back upriver, saw his ships sailing before him, and felt relieved that he was at the rear; if the Empire did catch up with them, Erec would be the first to defend his people.

"You need no longer worry, my lord," came a soft voice.

Erec felt a gentle, reassuring hand on his arm and he turned to see Alistair, coming up beside him and smiling graciously back.

"Our ships are faster than theirs," she said, "and there has been so sign of them all day. As long as we keep sailing, they shall not catch us."

Erec smiled back and kissed her, reassured by her presence, as always.

"There is always something a leader must worry about," he replied. "If it's not what's behind us, then it's what lies ahead."

"Of course," she replied. "All security is an illusion. As soon as we stepped foot on this ship and set sail from the Southern Isles, safety did not exist. But that's what ships are meant for, is it not? That is what makes us who we are."

Erec was impressed by her wisdom, her courage, and he knew that royal blood flowed through her. As he studied her, he noticed her beautiful blue eyes glistening, and he sensed something was different about her—he was not quite sure what. He felt as if she were withholding something from him.

She looked back at him questioningly.

"What is it, my lord?" she finally asked.

He hesitated.

"You seem...different these past days," he said. "I'm not sure how. I feel you are perhaps...withholding some secret from me."

Alistair blushed and looked away, and he felt sure that she was.

"It is... nothing, my lord," she said. "I am just distracted by the departure of my brother. I worry for Thorgrin, for Guwayne. And I wish to be reunited with our people again."

Erec nodded, and understood—though he was still not quite convinced.

"Erec!" suddenly shouted a voice, and Erec turned to see Strom beckoning him at the bow of the ship, agitated.

There was a sudden commotion as men rushed forward for the front of the ship, and Erec broke into action and raced across the deck, Alistair beside him.

Erec weaved his way between men until he finally reached the bow. Waiting for him was Strom, who handed him a long looking glass and pointed upriver.

"There," Strom said urgently, "to your right. That small speck."

Erec looked closely through the glass, holding it to his eye, the world moving up and down as they sailed through the current, and slowly, it came into view. It appeared to be a small Empire village, perched at the river's edge.

"It will be the first village we've encountered since entering this land," Strom said beside him. "They could be hostile."

Erec continued looking through the glass, taking it all in as they got neared, the wind carrying them closer with each passing moment. It was a quaint village, comprised of one-story clay houses, smoke rising from chimneys, children and dogs running about. Erec spotted women walking about casually, unafraid, and in the distance, men farming and a few fishing. From their dark skin and small stature, they appeared to be not of the Empire race; they seemed a peaceful people, perhaps under the Empire's subjugation.

Indeed, as Erec waited patiently for the current to carry them closer, he was surprised to see these people were of the human race—and as he looked closely, he spotted Empire taskmasters positioned throughout the village, holding whips. He watched a woman scream out as a taskmaster lashed her across the back, forcing her to drop her child.

Erec grew hot with indignation. He did a quick tally and counted perhaps a hundred Empire taskmasters spread throughout this village of several hundred peaceful folk.

He lowered the glass and handed it back to Strom, determined.

"Prepare your bows!" he shouted back to his men. "We sail into battle!"

His men cheered, clearly thrilled to be back into action, and they lined up along the rail and took positions high in the masts, bows and arrows at the ready.

"This is not our battle, my lord," said one of his commanders, coming up beside him. "Our battle awaits us far on the horizon. Should we not press on, and leave this village alone?"

Erec stood, hands on his hips, and shook his head.

"To sail onwards," he replied, "would be to turn our back on justice. That would make us less of who we are."

"But there is injustice everywhere, my lord," his commander countered. "Are we to be the knights for the world?"

Erec remained determined.

"Whatever is put before our eyes is put before there for a reason," he replied. "If we do not make an attempt to rectify it, then who are we?"

Erec turned to his men.

"Do not show yourselves until my command!" Erec yelled out.

His men quickly knelt, concealing themselves beneath the rail, preparing for the confrontation to come.

As their fleet of ships neared the village, rocking in the river's current, Erec sailed out in front, taking the lead—and soon, the villagers caught sight of him. The villagers began to stop what they were doing, farmers stood where they were, fishers began to pull back nets, all staring in surprise.

The Empire began to notice, too: one by one, Empire soldiers began to turn from their tasks and watch the river, looking curiously at Erec's ships. Clearly they had never seen their like before, and had no idea what to expect. Perhaps they assumed they were Empire ships?

Erec knew he had but a brief window of surprise until the Empire soldiers realized they were under attack—and he was determined to take advantage of it.

"Archers!" Erec shouted. "Introduce these Empire men to the strength of the Southern Isles!"

There arose a great cheer as Erec's men rose, as one, up from behind the rails, took aim, and sent a volley of arrows towards the shore.

The Empire soldiers turned to run—but they were not quick enough. The sky blackened with hundreds of arrows, arching high and descending, piercing the taskmasters one at a time.

They cried out, dropping their whips and swords where they stood, collapsing to the dirt, while terrified women and children screamed and fled.

"Anchors!" Erec cried out.

His fleet dropped their anchors, and they all followed Erec's lead as he jumped over the rail, flying through the air a good ten feet, landing in the water, up to his knees, then drawing his sword and charging on the sand.

As Erec led the charge to the village, Strom a foot behind him, dozens of Empire soldiers rushed forward to meet him, swords and shields at the ready.

The first sword slash came down, right for Erec's head. Erec blocked the blow with his shield, then swung around and slashed the soldier in the stomach. At the same moment he was attacked from the side, and he turned and slashed the other soldier before he could lower his sword, then turned the other way and kicked one back in the chest, sending him back, splashing in the water. He head-butted a fourth, breaking his nose, smashed another with his shield, and stabbed another in the chest.

Erec spun in every direction, a whirlwind, cutting through the ranks of hundreds of Empire soldiers. His men were close behind, and Strom, at his side, fought like a man possessed, felling soldiers left and right. Cries ran out in the morning air, and Erec lost more than one soldier, as more and more of these vicious Empire fighters seem to pour out of nowhere.

But Erec was filled with indignation at how these cruel taskmasters had treated the defenseless women and children, and he was determined to set things right and liberate this place, whatever the cost. He had also been eager, for far too long at sea, to let loose his aggression on the Empire, hand to hand, man to man, on dry land. It felt good to wield his sword again.

The sound of a whip cracked through the air, as an Empire soldier came at them from behind and lashed them with his long whip, catching Erec and Strom by surprise as he lashed the hilt of Erec's sword and yanked it from his hands. Erec reacted quickly, turning and throwing his shield sideways; it went spinning through the air and hit the soldier in the throat, knocking him down. Defenseless, another soldier brought his sword down for his face—but Strom stepped up and blocked the blow for his brother, then stabbed and killed the man.

Erec charged forward, ankles splashing in the water, grabbed his sword, extricated the whip, and kicked the taskmaster back, then stabbed him in the chest.

The fighting continued, on and on, thick and heavy, the waters running red with blood, men dying in every direction—until finally, it slowed. The clanging became less persistent, the smashing of shields dropped away, the sound of armor clinking died, as did the shouts and cries of men. Soon all that could be heard was the running of the river, thick in the air of silence.

Standing there, breathing hard, sweat running down the back of his neck, Erec looked about and surveyed the battlefield, and slowly, inwardly, he rejoiced as he saw his men standing over hundreds of Empire corpses, victorious. They all looked to him proudly, these great warriors of the Southern Isles, men he could not possibly be more proud to lead.

Slowly, like rabbits emerging from their holes, the villagers crept out of their houses, out of the village, coming forward in disbelief at the sight. They seemed hardly able to fathom that all the Empire taskmasters, these people who had oppressed them so badly, were dead.

Erec stepped forward and raised his sword and walked through the ranks of villagers, slicing the shackles holding them together—and all around him, his men did the same. He saw the villagers' eyes fill with tears as they dropped to their knees, liberated.

He looked down as one of them grabbed his leg, knelt, and cried. "Thank you," he wept. "Thank you."

CHAPTER THIRTEEN

Darius was rudely awakened, his head smashed into the iron bars of the carriage as it came to a grinding halt. He barely had time to process what was happening when keys jingled in the lock, the iron door slid open, and several rough hands grabbed him by the chest and yanked him out into harsh daylight.

He landed on the hard dirt ground, tumbling, dust rising all around him, squinting his eyes into the sun as he held up his hands. His ankles and wrists shackled, he couldn't resist even if he wanted to. The Empire taskmaster knew that, yet he placed his boot on Darius's throat anyway, enjoying inflicting pain on him. Darius could barely breathe, feeling his windpipe being crushed.

More rough hands grabbed him and yanked him to his feet and Darius shut his eyes again, every muscle in his body aching, feeling so stiff and sore, every movement hurting him.

"Move it, slave!" yelled a taskmaster, and Darius felt a rough shove as he stumbled forward through the streets.

Darius slowly opened his eyes into the glaring sun, trying to get his bearings and figure out where he was. At least that carriage had stopped; he could not stand another minute of its jolting his head.

Darius heard shouting all around him, and he realized he was in a crowded city, people bustling everywhere, slaves like him, chained by wrists and ankles, being ushered by Empire handlers in every direction. He was marched with a long group of slaves, dozens of them, all of them being ushered through a tall, arched stone opening, leading into a stone tunnel and toward what appeared to be a training barracks.

Darius heard a thunderous roar, and he glanced up and saw beyond that, a coliseum twice the size of the one in Volusia. It was the most glorious and terrifying thing he'd ever seen. And then he realized, without a doubt, where he was: he had arrived in the Empire capital.

Darius barely had time to consider it when he felt a club on his back.

"Move it, slave!" the man yelled out.

Darius went stumbling with the group into the darkened tunnel, and as he lost his balance and rushed forward, he felt a sharp sting as he was elbowed in his face.

"Don't bump me, boy!" snarled another slave in the darkness.

Darius, furious that a fellow slave would catch him off guard like that, would strike him for what was clearly an accident, reacted. He shoved the slave back, sending him stumbling backwards into a stone wall. He was so pent up with aggression that he had to let it out on someone.

The slave rushed forward to tackle Darius, but at that moment a new throng of slaves marched in, and it was so dark in here, the boy pounced on another slave, mistaking him for Darius. Darius heard the boys all shout out, as the two strangers wrestled on the ground. It went on for a few seconds before the taskmasters appeared with clubs and beat them both.

Darius kept moving with the others, and a moment later, he emerged into sunlight again and found himself in the dusty courtyard of a square, stone training barracks, its walls lined with arches all around. Lined up were hundreds of slaves, mostly boys his age, chained to each other by long shackles. Darius felt a rough hand on his wrist and he looked over as an Empire taskmaster clamped his shackles to another boy's

Darius continued shuffling into the courtyard in the long line of boys, hundreds of them lining the walls, until finally he felt a yank on his chain, and all the boys came to a stop, in a great clanging of chains.

Darius stood there in the tense silence, looking out with the others, wondering what to expect now. What agony awaited them next? he wondered.

A dozen Empire soldiers emerged from one of the arches, marching into the silent courtyard, a huge Empire soldier leading the way, clearly their leader. He paced up and down the line of boys, examining them one at a time.

Finally, scowling, he cleared his throat.

"You have all been brought here, to me, because you are the best of the best," he called out, his voice dark and malevolent. "You each hail from villages and towns and cities all over the Empire, from all four horns and both spikes. Every day, hundreds more of you are brought to me—yet only the best of you will fight in our coliseum."

All the boys remained silent, a thick tension in the air, as the taskmaster paced, his boots crunching on the ground.

"You might all be the best from wherever you are," he finally continued, "but that means nothing to me here. This is the greatest coliseum in the greatest capital in the world. Here you will find foes that will make your skills seem worthless. Most of you will die like dogs."

The taskmaster continued pacing and then, without warning, he drew his sword, stepped forward, and stabbed one of the boys in the heart.

The boy gasped and dropped to his knees, dead, yanking on the others' chains—and the other boys gasped. Darius, too, was shocked.

"That boy was weak," the taskmaster explained. "I could see it in his eyes. He did not stand tall enough."

Darius felt sickened as the taskmaster continued walking the line; he wanted to reach out and kill him—but he was chained, and weaponless.

A moment later, the taskmaster reached out and sliced a boy's throat, and the boy collapsed at his feet.

"That boy was too frail," he explained, as he continued walking.

Darius felt his heart pounding as the taskmaster neared him. Hardly twenty feet down from Darius, he swung his sword and cut off a boy's head.

Darius saw his head roll on the ground, and he looked up at the man, shocked that anyone could love killing so much.

"That boy," the taskmaster said, grinning a cruel grin and staring right at Darius, "I killed just for fun."

Darius reddened, enraged, feeling helpless.

The taskmaster turned to the others, and his voice boomed out:

"You are all nothing to me," he said. "Killing you is one of my great joys. There will be many more to take your place in the morning. You are truly worthless now."

Down the line the taskmaster went, trailed by his entourage, killing nearly every other boy, all in brutal ways. The boys, shackled, were defenseless; one tried to turn and run, but the taskmaster stabbed him in the back.

As they approached, Darius, sweating, no longer caring, filled with fury, forced himself to stand tall and strong. He stuck his chin up and stood as straight as he could, despite his wounds, staring defiantly straight ahead. If they would kill him then so be it; at least he would die proudly, not cowering like some of the others.

The taskmaster stopped before him and examined him as if he were an insect, sneering.

"You're not as big as the others," he said. "Or as muscular. I think we can do just fine without you."

He raised his sword and suddenly lunged at Darius, aiming to stab him in the heart.

Darius reacted. He had been prepared to stand there and die—indeed, would have welcome it—but something inside him took over, some warrior reflex that would just not let him die.

Darius sidestepped, raised his wrists, wrapped with shackles, and used his chains to catch the blade. He wrapped them up in it, then stepped aside and yanked hard, pulling the taskmaster toward him. He then leaned back and kicked the taskmaster in the solar plexus, sending him stumbling backwards, gasping and weaponless.

Darius sneered back and dropped his sword at his feet. It landed with a clang.

"You're going to have come at me with a lot better than that toothpick," Darius said, reveling in the moment.

The taskmaster stared back, shocked, and turned apoplectic. He grabbed a spare sword from the scabbard of the soldier beside him, then began to charge once again for Darius.

"I'm going to carve you into pieces," he said, "and leave your corpse for the dogs."

The man charged, but then stopped abruptly.

"No you're not," came a voice.

Darius was shocked to see a long staff suddenly drop down between him and the taskmaster, against the taskmaster's chest, holding him back.

The taskmaster scowled as he turned and looked over, and Darius was shocked to see a man standing there—a human—about his size and build, perhaps in his forties, his light-brown skin the same color as his, wearing only a simple brown robe and hood, and wielding only a staff. Even more amazing was that he held the Empire soldier back. Darius had no idea what a free human was doing here.

The man looked back at the taskmaster steadily, fearlessly, calmly, standing there proudly. His sleeves cut off, he was wiry and muscular, like Darius, but not overly so. He wore sandals, the laces wrapped up his shins to his knees, and he bore the proud face, square jaw, and noble look of a warrior.

"You will let this one be," the man ordered the taskmaster, his voice low and full of confidence.

The taskmaster sneered.

"Get that stick away from me," he replied, "or I will kill you along with him."

The taskmaster raised his sword and slashed at the staff, to cut it in two.

But the man moved quicker than any warrior Darius had never seen before, moving so quickly that he was able to move his staff out of the way and bring it down in a circle on the Empire soldier's wrists, smacking them so hard that he knocked the sword from his grip. It fell to the ground, and the man then held the tip of his staff to the stunned taskmaster's throat.

"I said, this boy will live," the man repeated firmly.

The taskmaster frowned.

"You may train them," the taskmaster said, "but it is I who decides who lives and who dies. You might be able to outfight me, but look around—here are dozens of my men, all with fine weaponry and armor. Are you going to stop all of them with that stick of yours?"

The man, to Darius's surprise, smiled and lowered his staff.

"We shall make a deal," he said. "If your dozen soldiers can disarm me, then the boy is yours. If I, however, can disarm all of them, then the boy is mine to train."

The taskmaster grinned back.

"They will do more than disarm you," he said. "They will kill you. And I'm going to enjoy watching you die."

The taskmaster nodded to his men, and with a shout they all raised their swords and charged the man.

Darius watched, riveted, his heart pounding for the man, desperate for him to live, as the man stood in the center of them all with only his long staff. He spun every which way as the men approached from all sides.

The man, as quick as lightning, swatted the sword from one soldier's hand after another. Darius had never seen anyone move that quickly, and he was a thing of beauty to watch, spinning and turning, ducking and tumbling, wielding his staff as if it were alive. He deflected one soldier's blow, then jabbed another soldier in the gut, disarming him. He swung around and smashed one in the temple, knocking him down; he poked another straight on, breaking his nose, while with another he swung upwards, knocking the sword from his hand—and with another, he swung low, sweeping his feet out from under him.

As other soldiers ran and swung for him, he jumped high in the air, missing one sword slash, then brought his staff straight down, jabbing the man in the back of the neck and felling him.

On and on he went, spinning and slashing and jabbing and ducking, a whirlwind, creating havoc in every direction and disarming one after the next, and then felling each one.

As he knocked down the last of them, he stepped forward and held the tip of his staff at the man's throat, pinning him to the ground. He slowly surveyed the battlefield, the dozen soldiers all disarmed, on their backs or hands and knees, groaning, and he looked over at the Empire taskmaster and grinned.

"I believe the boy is mine," he said.

The taskmaster turned and stormed away, and the man turned and met Darius's gaze. He was the most noble and skilled warrior Darius had ever laid eyes upon, and he felt in awe to be in his presence. It was the first time a man had ever risked his life for him, and he hardly knew what to say.

He didn't have time, though, because the mysterious man turned abruptly and disappeared into the crowd, leaving Darius baffled. Who was this man? And why would he risk his life for him?

CHAPTER FOURTEEN

Thor held tight to Lycoples's neck, gripping his rough scales as they soared through the air, exhilarated to be riding on the back of a dragon again. They tore through the air at full speed, the clouds whipping Thor in the face, as they raced for the pack of gargoyles on the horizon carrying Guwayne. Thor burned with determined to retrieve his son, so close now, finally, urging Lycoples on to ever greater speeds.

"Faster!" Thor prodded.

Lycoples flapped her wings again and again, lowering her head, equally determined to save Thor's son.

Thor felt elated to be riding with Mycoples and Ralibar's offspring—it made him feel as if he were back with Mycoples again. He had missed her terribly every day since she'd died, and riding with her offspring made him feel restored. There was also no more exhilarating feeling than flying through the air, moving at such speed, crossing oceans in days when it would take ships moons. It made him feel invincible once again. He felt light, as fast as a bird, with nothing left in the world to stand in his way.

Thorgrin also felt an intense connection with Lycoples, a very different energy than with her mother. Lycoples was much smaller, still young, half the size of a full-grown dragon, and she flew with an awkward passion, bounding through the air, not quite in full control of all her powers yet. Flying on her back, he felt new life coming into the world again, the birth of a new race unfolding before him.

Thorgrin also found himself easily able to share his thoughts and feelings with her, and he knew she sensed his urgency to find Guwayne. She flapped furiously without his needing to prod, going faster than he could ask her to. They flew so fast that he could barely catch his breath, dipping in and out of the clouds, closing in on the gargoyles. Thor clutched her scales while with his free hand he gripped the Sword of the Dead. He could feel it throbbing in his hand, eager for blood.

They began to close in, getting closer to the pack of gargoyles, now but a hundred yards away, and Thorgrin wondered where they were flying to, where they were so eager to take Guwayne. As he squinted he could see Guwayne, dangling from the claws of one of those creatures at the head of the pack. Were they really taking him to the Land of Blood? If so, why?

Thor looked out at the horizon and saw nothing but ocean as far as the eye could see; he saw no Land of Blood. Had Ragon been mistaken? Were those just the words of a dying man?

Suddenly, Thorgrin was surprised to see the huge flock of gargoyles split in two, half of them circling back and racing to confront him, while the other half continued on. As they approached he got a good look at them and could see they looked like enormous bats, with wide, slimy black wings, long claws, and fangs. They reared their narrow heads and screeched as they flew right for him.

Thor gripped his sword, eager to meet them in battle, and Lycoples, to her credit, did not waver in fear. Instead, she flew faster, and Thor, eager to set wrongs right, raised the Sword of the Dead high. It was so heavy, ten times the weight of any other sword, yet somehow it felt perfect in his hands. Its black blade glistened in the sky, and as the monsters screeched, Thor replied with a battle cry of his own. He would cut through all of them to retrieve his son.

As the first of the gargoyles reached him, raising its fangs for Thor's face, Thor reached down and slashed the sword, slicing it in half. Its blood sprayed everywhere, as the gargoyle tumbled through the air, past him.

Another came at him, then another, approaching from all sides, and Thor turned and slashed in every direction, ducking and slicing them in half. He cut off the talons of one, the wings of another, then ducked as he was scratched on the shoulder by a third—and reached up and thrust his sword into its exposed belly.

The swarm of gargoyles descended on him, and Thor fearlessly met their embrace, fighting like a man possessed, a man with nothing left to lose. The Sword of the Dead fought, too, coming to life, like a living being in his hand. It whizzed and hummed and led the way, urging Thor on, leading him to slash and thrust and block blows. It was like having a fighting partner in his hand. The Sword hummed and sang as it sliced through the air, leaving a trail of blood and severed gargoyles in its wake, all of them tumbling down to the ocean far below.

Lycoples, too, joined in, lashing out with her talons at all gargoyles who dared attack her. She was young, but vicious—and fearless. She raised her razor-sharp talons and slashed gargoyles left and right, reaching them before they reached her and slicing them in half. She reached out and grabbed others by their heads and squeezed to death, while still others she grabbed and threw, hurling them down through the air, to the ocean. Others still she bit, opening her huge jaws and sinking her teeth into their scales as they shrieked out in pain.

Finally, as a fresh swarm came at them, Lycoples threw back her head, screeched, and let out a stream of flames. Her flame was not as strong yet as her parents', yet still it was strong enough to wreak havoc: the dozens of remaining gargoyles, engulfed in the flames, let out an awful shriek as they were immersed in the cloud of fire, their horrible screams filling the air as they tumbled down, aflame, to the sea below.

Thor was taken aback by Lycoples's power, not expecting such a stream of flame, and the few gargoyles who remained alive also looked back with scared expressions—and a whole new fear of Lycoples. They turned and flew off into the horizon, catching up with the other half of their flock.

"Faster, Lycoples, faster!" Thor cried out, lowering his head and holding on tight as she, enraged, flew at an even greater speed.

Lycoples needed no prodding. She tore through the air faster than Thor could breathe, and they dove in and out of clouds, the scarlet sun beginning to set as they bore down on the gargoyles. The gargoyles dared not turn to face them now, but rather flew with all their speed, flapping their wings furiously to try to get away.

As they approached, Thor could finally see Guwayne again, up ahead—and his heart beat faster. He was so close now, nothing would get in his way. He would slaughter each and every one of these creatures, and soon they would be reunited again.

As Thor glanced up at the horizon, he did a double take, shocked by the sight before him. On the horizon, there slowly appeared what seemed to be a waterfall in the sky. It stretched in every direction, as far as he could see, a wall of running water—stained red. It ran from the heavens, right down to the oceans, so thick he could not see through it, and he heard a great roaring noise as he came closer. He began to realize what it was: a waterfall of blood.

Thorgrin suddenly knew, without a doubt, that it was a barrier, a wall blocking off another world: the entry to The Land of Blood. And as he saw all gargoyles heading for it, he suddenly realized where they were going—and realized that it might provide them safe harbor.

"FASTER!" he cried.

Lycoples managed to fly even faster, closing in on them, fifty yards away, then thirty, then ten…. The waterfall loomed before them, the noise now deafening.

The gargoyles flew just a bit too fast, and as Thor neared them, they all suddenly entered the waterfall of blood, disappearing into it.

Thor braced himself, too, preparing to enter after them—but suddenly, to his surprise, Lycoples stopped short in the air, rearing her head, refusing to enter it. Thor could not understand what was going on. It was as though Lycoples were scared to enter.

She flapped her wings, hanging there, arching her back, screeching, and Thor realized that, for some reason, she could not pass through this magical barrier to the Land of Blood. Thor reddened, realizing the gargoyles knew that all along.

Lycoples, frustrated, screeched again and again, clearly wanting to enter and frustrated that she could not.

Thor felt his heart breaking as he watched the gargoyles disappear into the waterfall with his son, disappearing from view.

Thor thought quickly. He looked down and scanned the ocean, and he saw in the distance, on the horizon, his Legion brothers, following in their ship. Thor directed Lycoples back down, across the ocean, toward his friends, knowing he had no choice. If Lycoples could not enter the Land of Blood, then Thor would have to enter without her.

Lycoples flew Thor down to the ship, and as she dove low and slowed, Thor jumped off her back and onto the deck. He stood there, looking up at her, and she flapped her wings, disappointed, wanting him to ride her again.

Thor shook his head.

"No, Lycoples," he said to her. "You can be of no use to me where I need to go. You can help me elsewhere: go find my beloved.

Find Gwendolyn, wherever she is. Tell her I live. Guwayne lives. And save her for me from whatever danger she might be in."

Lycoples screeched and hovered, clearly not wanting to leave Thor's side.

"GO!" Thor commanded firmly.

Lycoples finally, reluctantly, turned and flew off, disappearing in the horizon.

All the others gathered around Thor on the ship and stared at him, stunned. He looked out, past the bow, to the looming waterfalls of blood, and knew what he had to do.

"Brothers and sisters," he said, "tonight we enter the Land of Blood."

CHAPTER FIFTEEN

Gwendolyn walked side-by-side with the Queen, escorting her across the golden skywalk that spanned the capital of the Ridge. The path was made of solid gold cobblestones, elevated fifteen feet above the city streets, spanning from the castle exit to all corners of the city. It was a walkway reserved for royals, and as they walked the Queen's servants trailed behind them, holding up parasols to block the sun.

The two strolled arm-in-arm, the Queen affectionately linking arms with her and insisting that she take her on a tour of the city. The Queen fondly showed Gwen all the sights as they went, pointing out notable architecture and orienting her to the various neighborhoods of this ancient city. Gwendolyn felt comforted by her presence, especially after such a long stretch without female company. In some respects, the Queen was like the warm mother that she never had.

It made Gwendolyn reflect on her own mother. Her mother had been a cold and hard Queen, always deciding based on what was right for the kingdom—but not necessarily what was right for their family. She had also been a cold, hard mother, and Gwendolyn had had endless arguments and power struggles with her. Gwendolyn recalled the first time she had met Thorgrin, her mother's epic struggle to keep the two of them apart. It brought back fresh bitterness and resentment.

It also caused Gwen think of other times, other places; she recalled the balls in her father's court, everyone dressed in their finest, the jousts, the festivals, the endless years of bounty and good times, years Gwen was certain could never end. She recalled the first time she had ever met Thorgrin, back in the bounty of the Ring, just a young, naïve boy entering King's Court for the first time. It felt like another lifetime. She felt so aged since then, so much upended in her life. Even here, within the splendor of this place, she had a hard time imagining days of comfort and security like that coming back to her again.

Gwen snapped out of it as the Queen pulled her along and pointed up ahead.

"This quarter is where most of our people live," the Queen said proudly.

Gwendolyn looked down at the beautiful city, afforded a sweeping view from up here on the skywalk, and was in awe at its beauty and sophistication. The city was crammed with pristine houses of every shape and size, some built of marble, others limestone, all snuggled in close together, giving the city a cozy feel. The city looked perfectly worn, crisscrossed by cobblestone streets, horses walking through, slowly pulling carriages through the streets. Lining the streets were people selling their wares, and everywhere there was the smell of food: stalls were overflowing with massive fruits, while vendors sold sacks and barrels of wine. Other shops were everywhere, tanners selling hides, blacksmiths weaponry, and jewelers sparkling gems. Everyone was dressed in their finest, and they strolled about this luxurious city in harmony.

Gwen looked up and saw the impressive fortifications walling in the city, its ancient stone walls lined with knights, their armor gleaming in the sun. She saw the castle towering over the city, like a watchman, its ramparts staggered and lined with more knights, beacons of strength and perfect discipline. Church bells tolled softly in the distance, dogs barked below in the streets and children squealed in delight as they ran after them. A gentle breeze, heavy with moisture from the lakes, caressed her as she walked, and Gwen realized this place was as close to perfection as one could imagine. In the distance, the waters glistened and in the far distance, the peaks of the Ridge loomed over all of them, a faint outline on the horizon, shrouded in mist, making this place feel even more protected.

Gwen saw people open and closing their shutters, hanging clothes out to dry, and as she glanced down, she noticed many people waving up at them affectionately. She felt too elitist walking up here, on this pathway.

"You are distracted, dear Queen," the Queen said to her, smiling.

Gwen blushed.

"Excuse me," she said. "It's just that…I prefer to interact with my people. I like to embrace them, to walk the same streets as they."

Gwen hoped she hadn't offended her, and she was relieved to see the Queen's smile widen.

"You are a girl after my own heart," she said. "I was hoping you would ask. I don't like to live as royals do, either—I would rather be with my people."

She led her down a curved, golden staircase, into the streets, and as they descended, there was an excited rush amongst her people; they all gushed at the Queen's presence and rushed forward to greet her, handing her fruits and flowers. Gwen could see how loved she was by her people—and she understood why: she was the kindest Queen she'd ever met.

Gwen enjoyed walking the streets, loved the vitality, the smells of cooking meat stronger down here; it was bustling with people, and she loved the energy of this place. These people of the Ridge, she was coming to realize, were warm and friendly people, quick to smile and to embrace strangers. She was beginning to feel at home.

"Our walking through the street is, in fact, most convenient. My daughter whom you wish to see is on the far end of the city, perched in her library. This is the quickest way to get there."

Gwen thought of where they were going—the Royal Library—which she so badly wished to see, and she grew excited. She also thought of the Queen's youngest daughter, whom the King asked her to see first, and she wondered once again about her.

"Tell me about her," Gwen said.

The Queen's face lit up at the mention of her.

"She's remarkable," she said. "She has a mind unlike anyone I've ever met. You will see that there is really no one like her. I don't know where she gets it from—certainly not from me."

The Queen shook her head as she spoke, her eyes watering with admiration.

"How can it be that a ten-year-old girl can have an intellect powerful enough to be the scholar of the kingdom? Not only is she the fastest thinker I've ever met, but she retains scholarship unlike anyone I've ever met. It's more than an affinity—it's an obsession. Ask her anything about our history, and she will tell you. I'm ashamed to say her knowledge is greater even than mine. And yet, I am so proud of her—she spends all her days in that library. It is making her far too pale, if you ask me. She should be out, playing with her friends."

Gwen thought of it all as she walked, remembering her first meeting her at the feast, and how taken she had been by her. Clearly, this was an extraordinary girl. Being so enamored of books, the two of them had clicked instantly, as Gwen had sensed a kindred soul in her. It made Gwen think of her time spent in the House of Scholars, and she knew that if her father had not intervened, she would have spent all her days locked away in that building, lost in books.

"Your husband told me I must see her first," Gwen said. "He said I should ask her of the history before visiting the tower and your other son, Kristof. He said she would give me a primer, a better understanding of it."

Gwen watched the Queen's face darken at the mention of her other son. She nodded sadly.

"Yes, she will tell you all about that cursed tower and more," she said. "Though I don't know what good it will do. My children in that tower are lost to me now."

Gwen looked at her, stunned.

"Children?" she repeated. "The king mentioned but one son. Have you others?"

The Queen looked down as they walked, cutting through the streets, passing vendors, and she remained silent for a very long time. Just when Gwen began to wonder if she would ever answer, finally, the Queen wiped a tear and looked at her, her face filled with sadness.

"My daughter lives there, too."

Gwen gasped.

"A daughter? Your husband did not mention it."

The Queen nodded.

"Kathryn. He never mentions her. He acts as if she does not exist. Just because she is touched."

Gwen looked back, puzzled.

"Touched?" she echoed.

The Queen looked away, and Gwen realized it was too painful for her to discuss it, and she did not want to pry. A silence fell back over them as they walked, Gwen more curious than ever. These people of the Ridge seemed to hold endless secrets. It made Gwen think of the Queen's other son, Mardig, and made her wonder what darkness lay in their family.

They weaved their way throughout the streets and finally turned a corner, and as they did, the Queen came to an abrupt stop. She looked up, and Gwen did, too.

Gwen gasped, in awe at the building before her. It was a building unlike any Gwen had ever seen, built of shining marble, with huge golden doors shaped in a tall arch, intricately carved. The doors were adorned with golden images of books carved into them, and long, tapered stained-glass windows lined the exterior. It resembled a church but was more circular in shape, and even more impressive, set in the midst of an open city square with nothing around it in every direction, encircled by a circular courtyard of clean, golden cobblestone. Gwen could see right away the respect that this city had for books, for scholarship; after all, this Royal Library sat like a beacon in the center of the city.

"My daughter awaits you inside," the Queen said, a sadness now to her voice. "Ask her anything you will. She will tell you all. There are some things that are too painful for a mother to speak of."

She gave Gwendolyn a quick hug, then turned and disappeared in the streets, followed by her servants.

Gwen, alone, faced the huge golden doors, twenty feet high, a foot thick, and as she reached out and laid a hand on their golden handles, she pulled, and felt ready to enter another world.

*

As Gwen entered the Royal Library, waiting to greet her was Jasmine, standing there alone in the vast hall of marble, her hands before her, lightly clasped at her waist, and staring back with a sweet, excited smile, intelligence shining in her eyes.

She rushed forward, beaming, and took Gwen's hand.

"I've been waiting and *waiting* for you!" she exclaimed, as she turned and excitedly began to give Gwen a tour. "My dad said you would be coming this morning, and I've waited ever since. I must have checked the windows a hundred times. Did my mom take you on one of her long and boring tours?" she asked with a short laugh, delighting herself.

Gwen could not help but laugh, too, this child's enthusiasm infectious. She was captivated by Jasmine from the moment she saw her, so intelligent and endearing. She was also talkative and fun. There was a bounce to her step, a playful giddiness which Gwendolyn did not expect. She expected her to be serious and somber, lost in books, like any other scholar—but she was anything but. She was like any other child, carefree, skipping along, joyous, warm and good-natured. In some ways, she reminded Gwendolyn of the carefree, joyous spirit she'd once had herself as a youth. She wondered when, exactly, she lost it.

As Jasmine led her through the halls, her talking never ceasing, she moved from one topic to the next with surprising dexterity, pointing out one rack of books after the other.

"This stack on the right are the tragedies of our first playwright, Circeles," she said. "I consider them to be basically trite works, what you might expect from the first generation of Ridge playwrights. Of course, they were suited for different occupations back then—mostly martial. As Keltes says, with each generation comes a refinery, a move from martial to higher skills. We all strive for higher forms of grace, do we not?"

Gwen looked back at her, dazzled by her speech, her nonstop flow of words and knowledge, as she continued relentlessly, pointing out rack after rack of books. They passed through endless corridors, decorated with ornate wall paintings, their floors lined with gold.

The library was like a maze, and Jasmine led her down winding, narrow corridors lined with books on either side. The racks of books, made of gold, rose twenty feet high, and all the books looked ancient, leather-bound, penned, Gwendolyn could see, in the ancient language of the Ring. There were a staggering number of books, even for someone like Gwendolyn, and amazingly, Jasmine seemed to recognize every single one.

"And here we have the histories, of course," Jasmine continued, pulling down a book as she walked and leafing through it. "They stretch for miles. It's organized from the early historians through the latter ones—it should, in fact, be the other way around. You'd think the latter would stand upon the shoulders of the former, offer a more enlightened perspective into the history of the Ridge and the Ring— but that's not so. As is often the case, the original historians were better versed than any who followed. I think there's some truth to the notion that latter generations outdo the former—yet there is more truth to the notion of former generations holding ancient wisdom untouchable by the latter ones," she said. "The firstborn syndrome, is it?"

Gwen's mind spun in a flurry, trying to process everything she was saying, and she could not help but feel as if she were speaking to an eighty-year-old. This dynamo of a girl held the wisdom of Aberthol and Argon combined, but with a speed and energy to her that left Gwen dizzy. Gwen realized right away that she was outmatched by this young girl's intelligence and scholarship—and it was the first time she had ever felt that way before, with anyone. It was both intimidating and exhilarating.

"You're a reader, too," Jasmine said, as she turned a corner, leading them down yet another twisting corridor of books. "I saw it in your face the moment I met you. You're like me. Except you were burdened with your Queenship. I understand. It must have been awful. No more time to read, I presume. It is probably the worst part of being Queen. You probably love it here."

Gwen smiled.

"How do you do that?" Gwen said. "You read my mind."

The girl laughed back, giddy.

"It's easy to spot another reader. There's a distant look to your eyes, as if you're lost in another world. A telltale sign. You live in a heightened world, more glorious than our own, as do I. It is a world of fantasy. A world of beautiful drama, where everything is possible, where the only limits are our imagination."

Jasmine sighed.

"Our world, here and now, is so pedestrian," she added. "Blacksmiths and butchers and hunters and warriors and knights— how dreadfully inane. All they want to do is kill one another, outmatch each other at jousting contests and the like. Dreadful. Redundant, too."

She sighed, turning down yet another corridor.

"Books, on the other hand," she continued, "are infinite. Reading a book, if you ask me, is more chivalrous than killing a man. And it offers a much more interesting world to explore. It's a pity our society values the killers over the scholars. After all, without us readers, how would the armorer know how to forge the armor? The blacksmith to hammer the sword? How would the cobbler know how to mend horseshoes, or the engineer to build a catapult? And how would the King know whom he fought against if he was unable to read, unable to, at the very least, identify the banner on the far side of the battlefield? How would his men know who to kill?

"Knights do not fight in a void," she continued. "They are more indebted to us readers, to our books, than they'd ever care to admit. I would posit that a warrior needs books to survive, much more so than weapons."

She hurried down a flight of steps, Gwen right behind her trying to keep up.

"And yet, here we are, treated like third-rate citizens, relegated to our libraries. Thank god I'm a girl. If I were a boy, I'd be wasting my time right now on the battlefield, and missing out on all of this."

She turned a corner, stopped, and gestured dramatically, and Gwen looked out at a room that took her breath away. Gwen found herself standing in a vast chamber, its ceilings soaring a hundred feet high, shaped in a huge circle, with marble columns stretched out every thirty feet, and steps leading down to a shining marble floor set with dozens of golden tables. On each of these tables lay heaps and heaps of books, of every size and shape, some as big as an entire table. The room was lit by an endless array of candle chandeliers, decorated with crystal.

Gwen stood there, in awe at the sight, while Jasmine bounded happily into it, clearly comfortable here, as if it were her personal living room.

"This is the main reading room," she explained as she went, Gwen slowly following, taking it all in. "Sometimes I like to hide away in small nooks and crannies when I read—but most of my time I spend reading in here. This place is empty all the time anyway, so it doesn't really matter where I read. But sometimes, reading in different rooms makes you feel differently about a book, don't you think?"

Gwen looked out at all the tables, confused.

"I don't understand," she said. "If no one uses this room but you, what are all those books on all those different tables? It looks as if an army uses this room every day."

Jasmine laughed in delight.

"Does it?" she replied. "Sorry. I know I'm messy. I'm not good at putting away my books."

Gwen stared at her, dumbfounded.

"Are you saying that you alone are reading all these books?" she asked in disbelief, looking out at the hundreds of volumes spread out over a dozen tables, all open, in some state of use.

Jasmine smiled.

"It's not that many," she replied, demure. "These are just my favorites. I've actually resolved to read far more this year."

Jasmine bounded from table to table, forgetting Gwendolyn, already preoccupied by the books before her. She practically dove into the room, rushing to the closest table, grabbing a huge book and scanning through the pages. Gwen watched in disbelief as Jasmine flipped through the pages with lightning speed. Gwen had never seen anyone read that fast. Jasmine was humming to herself as she read, lost in the book, as if she forgot Gwen was in the room.

In just moments, she finished it.

She turned to Gwen, a smile on her face.

"One of the less dull histories," Jasmine said, sighing. "I really delve into histories, but I knew you were coming, and knew you'd want to know, and I wanted to be prepared. I assume, of course, you want to know everything about the history of the Ring, about our shared ancestors. That is human nature after all, isn't it? Don't people always want to know about themselves?"

Jasmine looked back with a twinkle in her eye and Gwen smiled, her mind spinning with all of Jasmine's words, still trying to take it all in. She reached over and laid a hand on her shoulder.

"You are a startling, amazing human being," was all Gwen, speechless, could say. "If I were to ever have a daughter, I wish she would be just like you."

For the first time, Jasmine relaxed, beaming with pride, and she hurried over and gave Gwen a quick hug. Then she turned and went back to her books, opening a new one.

Gwen came over, leaned over her, and began to read over her shoulder. This book, oversized and leather-bound, was penned in the ancient language of the Ring, and luckily, it was a language Gwen could understand well, having been drilled into her since birth by Aberthol and others. Gwen felt thrilled to be here, in this still, sacred house of books. She could sit in this library forever, shut out all the woes of the world. There was nothing she would like more.

Yet as she tried to read, Jasmine turned the pages so quickly, it was hard for Gwen to keep up with her.

Jasmine quickly finished it, shut it, reached over, and took out another book.

"I'll spare you the monotony of it," Jasmine said. "The essence of that book is that the ancestors of Ridge and the Ring were shared. But you know that already. That book focuses more on the parting of them. Relatively dull stuff."

"Tell me," Gwen said, eager to know.

Jasmine shrugged, as if it were all common knowledge.

"At one point, perhaps seven centuries ago, there was a parting of the ways. A mass exodus from the Ridge. Your side of the family left here, crossed the Great Waste, and somehow made or found ships and crossed the sea. Of course there was an Empire pursuit, and many of your people died, either in the Waste, the jungles, or at sea. Many of those who first arrived in the Ring, too, did not survive. Most were killed in what I believe you call 'The Wilds.'"

Gwen stared back, astounded at the history.

"Yes," Gwen said. "The land beyond the Canyon, on the outer edge of the Ring."

Jasmine nodded.

"The main challenge your people faced was building a bridge to span the Canyon. The first bridge was the Western Crossing. Three more were to follow. It took a thousand workers a thousand days to carve the rock. The beasts tried to cross, too, but your people were able to guard the bridge. Other beasts descended the Canyon to climb up the other side—but the theories were they were killed by the creatures who lived down below."

Gwen listened, riveted, her mind swimming with questions but not wanting to interrupt.

Jasmine sighed.

"Of course, for those who made it," she continued, "the original Ring was no easy place. It was filled with savage monsters in and of itself, its land was wild, and its Highlands insurmountable. Almost at once, there was a divide between the Western and Eastern provinces, which I believe evolved into the Western and Eastern kingdoms. The East was less fertile, more arid, and its climate more harsh. Savage tribes lived there, whom, I believe, formed the basis of the Eastern Kingdom.

"It was only once your people could secure the Canyon that things changed. And that, in turn, leads back to what mattered most in perhaps all of your history: the history of the Shield. And of the Destiny Sword. Without the Shield, the Ring was just another indefensible place, another island, a place as insecure and hostile as the rest of the world. But it was the first great sorcerers whose magic forged the Shield, that laid the groundwork for your people's survival."

Gwen had never been so immersed in a story; she had read histories her entire life, yet never had heard any of this. She wondered what precious volumes they had here in the Ridge that her people lacked in the Ring.

"Tell me more," Gwendolyn said.

Suddenly, church bells rang out, muted, from somewhere outside the walls, and Jasmine looked up, distracted for the first time. Gwendolyn saw her expression darken, and wondered why.

"I can't stand their sound," she said. "They toll incessantly."

Gwen was confused.

"Why? Who rings them? Are they not church bells?"

Jasmine shook her head.

"I wish," she replied. "They are the bells of the tower. The bells of the false religion, the cult who hold my brother and sister hostage. Not physically, of course, but intellectually, spiritually—and those bonds are worse than shackles. I love them both dearly, and I would give anything to have them back."

Jasmine had suddenly switched topics, had forgotten about the history of the Destiny Sword and the Shield, and Gwen realized something about her: her attention span was limited. Her mind worked so fast that she changed topics with an alarming dexterity. She was brilliant, but she was scattered. Gwen still wanted desperately to know more about the Shield and the Destiny Sword—but she would leave it for another time. After all, she had come to her to begin with at the King's request, to find out more about the tower.

"Tell me about your siblings," Gwendolyn said, eager to know more.

"What did Mother and Father tell you?" she asked.

"Not much," she replied.

Jasmine shook her head.

"Of course not. They fear what they do not know and are ashamed of what they do not understand. Like most people. Provincial, wouldn't you say?"

Gwen looked back, not really understanding.

"My brother," she continued, "has been brainwashed. He was always zealous in all his passions, and unfortunately, they found the wrong subject. My sister, well…that is more complex. She was born the way she is. She has always been lost to us, in her own way. But now—she is amongst them."

Gwen struggled to understand.

"She's catatonic," Jasmine explained, seeing Gwen's confused expression. "She stares out the window, doesn't speak a word. Ever since birth. Our *noble* people of the Ridge, with their culture of perfection, or warriors and knights and all that nonsense—are ashamed of her. Sickening, really. It is my parents' greatest shortcoming, if you ask me. Anyone who is not perfect is considered a threat to our society. But I love my sister dearly—I always have. I always found a way to communicate with her. She has her way, too—you just have to be open to hearing her."

Gwen began to understand, and felt sadness for them all.

"Your father asked me to visit them," Gwen said. "To try to get them back."

"A lost cause," Jasmine sighed. "You cannot travel the canals of the mind."

"But he also thinks the Tower holds a clue. That it is guarding something—some ancient knowledge, some secret history."

Jasmine sighed and looked away, and for the first time she fell silent for a very long time, looking off into the distance with glassy eyes, as if debating something monumental.

"That rumor has persisted for centuries," she said. "Many believe the Light Seekers hide the lost books. These are books I've never seen—I have never even seen proof of their existence. I begged my brother many times, and my sister: if they exist, I'd give anything to read them. But they insist that they do not—or at least, they've never seen them. And even if they do, even if they are hidden somewhere in the bowels of the tower, who is to say whether they really contain the great remedy for our destiny that all expect them to?"

She sighed.

"This is just another of my father's dreams," she continued. "Perhaps it has something to do with his age? His yearning for the return of his children?"

Gwendolyn looked away, feeling disappointed by the entire conversation, trying to absorb it all. Jasmine's knowledge was dizzying, and Gwen figured it would take months to fully understand everything she was saying. It was the first time she had ever felt this way, so in over her head intellectually, and it was unsettling experience.

Jasmine must have sensed her sadness, because she looked over at her compassionately, and laid a hand on her wrist.

"Enough of the Tower," she said. "You will go there and see for yourself. But I have seen in your eyes what is really troubling you. Thorgrin and Guwayne, is that right?"

Gwen looked at her, hope in her eyes, wondering how she knew.

"Has Argon not told you anything?" Jasmine asked.

Gwen looked at her, confused.

"Argon?" she echoed. "Tell me what? He is sick. He is unresponsive."

Jasmine shook her head.

"No longer," she replied. "Our healers are very fine at what they do. His healing has begun. He is conscious even now."

Gwendolyn looked back at her, filled with hope, elated.

"How do you know?" she asked, baffled.

Jasmine smiled.

"Everything that happens in this court is carried by raven. I am known to be quite inquisitive."

Gwen studied her, amazed.

"What is it that Argon knows?" Gwen asked.

"The ancient ones," Jasmine said, "they hold a great many secrets, from the beginning of time. Also great knowledge, of which they do not speak."

She looked closely at Gwendolyn.

"Speak to Argon," she said. "Ask him about Thorgrin. About Guwayne. Ask him what he's withholding. I am sure it will surprise even   you."

CHAPTER SIXTEEN

Kendrick braced himself as the sharp claws of the tree clinger swooped down for his face with dizzying speed. The creature had leapt from the twisted tree so quickly, lunging down at him before Kendrick even had a chance to respond. Its claws were as long as its body, sharp and razor thin, and the beast, resembling a large sloth, with a hairy body, yellow beady eyes and sharp fangs, was out for blood. Clearly it had trapped many unsuspecting travelers under this tree before.

Kendrick knew that in a moment he would be decapitated, and his final thought, before it reached him, was what a shame it would be to die here, in the middle of nowhere, far from Gwendolyn and everyone he knew and loved.

As Kendrick braced himself there came a sudden clang of metal, and Kendrick saw Brandt, standing beside him, blocking the claws of the creature with his sword. At the same moment Atme stepped forward and plunged his sword straight through the creature's heart.

It let out an awful shriek and coughed up a yellow substance onto Kendrick as it collapsed down to the desert floor, dead.

Suddenly, the sky became filled with the awful screeches of these things. They sounded like a chorus of monkeys as they dove from the tree, their long claws sweeping through the air, dozens of them descending for the group of men.

Kendrick, grateful to Brandt and Atme for saving his life, broke into action, determined to repay the favor. He watched one of the beasts leap, claws extended, for Brandt's back, and he shoved Brandt aside, stepped forward, and threw his sword. It hurled end over end through the air before piercing the creature in the chest. It collapsed to the ground right before it reached Brandt, dead.

Kendrick spotted another beast out of the corner of his eye, coming for Atme, and he spun, drew his other short sword and slashed it midair, chopping off its head before it could sink its fangs into the back of his friend's neck.

A shriek filled the air and Kendrick wheeled to see one of the Silver cry out as a creature clung to his back and dug its teeth into the back of his shoulder. Kendrick rushed forward and used the hilt of his sort to butt it in its face, knocking it off—then he spun around and slashed another one as it sliced its claws at a Silver's face.

All around him his men followed his lead, breaking into action. They slashed at the creatures, fighting them one at a time as they all dove down. They felled them, but they also took cuts and bites in the process. The creatures were just too fast to fend off. The battle was bloody; for every creature they killed, one of his men took a dreadful cut. Those who were thickly armored wisely used it to their advantage, raising gauntlets and shields to block the blows.

Kendrick swung around with his gauntlet and smashed a creature before it reached him; he then raised his shield, swung it in a wide arc, and smashed three more in the air. For a moment he felt optimistic—but then he looked up and saw a seemingly endless supply of these creatures still falling from the twisted tree. They had stumbled right into a nest of these things, and clearly, these creatures were not used to letting visitors go without paying a deadly price. He knew something had to be done. His men were taking too many cuts, and at this rate, they would become too weakened to win.

Kendrick thought quickly, and he remembered his long flail in his saddle, the one he reserved for tournaments; it had an extra-long chain, fifteen feet, with three studded metal balls at the end. It was a deadly weapon, one he wielded rarely in battle, as there was a danger it could get tangled. But in a situation like this, it was exactly what he needed.

Kendrick snatched it, its long chain rattling as he swung it high overhead, spinning around and ready to inflict damage. But no sooner had he raised it when he felt a searing pain on the back of his shoulder and heard a screech in his ear. He felt the weight of one of these creatures landing on him, clinging to his back, sinking its fangs into his shoulder, its hot breath in his ear. He tried to grab it, but could not reach it.

Kendrick screamed out in agony, dropping to his knees, when just as quickly, his agony was relieved. Squealing, the creature went flying off him. Kendrick looked up to see Koldo, holding a sword, the creature impaled in it, dead.

Kendrick, grateful to him, wasted no time. He stood at full height and swung his flail in a wide arc, aiming high so as not to hit his own people. The three studded balls whistled as they swung through the air and impacted with several creatures; it tore them open with a splat, its razor-sharp spikes piercing their flesh. The creatures dropped from the air and fell to the ground, one of them killed right before it could land on Koldo's back.

Kendrick turned and swung his flail in wider and wider circles, again and again, rushing into the thick of men and knocking the creatures from the sky. Their screeches filled the air as he felled them one at a time, in each direction, falling like flies.

Soon, a pile of carcasses lay at his feet.

Kendrick looked out at the battlefield and saw Naten crying out, dropping his sword. Two creatures were on him, one biting his wrist and another his neck. A third lunged for his face. Kendrick knew that in another second, he'd be dead.

For a moment Kendrick hesitated, recalling how poorly Naten had treated him. But then he shook off his hesitation—his code of honor compelled him to save him, no matter how he had behaved. Kendrick would fight to the death for anyone he fought with, whether they deserved it or not.

Kendrick rushed forward to save Naten's life, swinging with all his might; his aim was true, and he managed to smash the creatures off of him, one at a time, with each swing. Realizing he wouldn't kill them all in time, Kendrick switched hands with his flail, drew his short spear with his free hand and threw it. It soared through the air and pierced the creature aiming for Naten's face, saving him just in time.

A great screeching filled the skies and all the creatures, in one coordinated action, began to retreat, lifting up into the sky, back into the twisted tree, like crows, clustering high in the branches. They made odd chirping strange noises as they all sat there, looking down on Kendrick and his flail, filled with hesitation.

A stillness fell over the battlefield, as Kendrick's men took stock and nursed their wounds, groaning from the bites and scratches. No one had escaped unscathed.

As Kendrick looked over at the men of the Ridge, he observed something different in their eyes this time: respect. These men of the

Ridge, once so wary of him, now looked at him differently. He had earned their respect.

All except for one.

Naten just stared back coldly, then turned his back and walked away. It was a strange gratitude, Kendrick thought, for saving his life.

Koldo and Ludvig came up beside him.

"You fought bravely," Koldo said. "You men of the Ring have proved your worth."

"You saved our men's lives on this day," Ludvig chimed in.

"Not quite," countered a dark voice.

Kendrick turned to see Naten standing there, frowning down at a corpse.

"He did not save his," he added.

Kendrick spotted a dead soldier, a man of the Ridge he did not recognize, lying there, his armor bloody, his eyes open, staring at the sky, covered in one too many scratches and bites.

"We shall bury him with all honors," Kendrick said, saddened by the loss.

Naten glared at him.

"We don't bury our dead, stranger," Naten snapped. "Not in the Ridge. We bring each and every one back for holy burning inside the Ridge. And do not forget: he would not be dead if it weren't for you."

Kendrick, taken aback by his coldness, watched as the other soldiers picked up the corpse and draped him sideways over a horse. The chirping of the creatures was reaching a new crescendo, and Kendrick looked up at them; they glared down menacingly.

"The sweepers are all attached," Koldo announced. "It's time to turn back."

As they all mounted their horses, one of Naten's men looked back up over his shoulder at the shaking tree.

"Tree Clingers," he said gravely, shaking his head. "A bad omen. Our mission is cursed."

"Nothing is cursed," Ludvig snapped.

"It is cursed, my lord," he said. "This was supposed to be a routine mission, to cover the trail. Now here we are, all of us wounded, one of us dead. You know as well as I do, we will never make it back to the Ridge again."

As Kendrick sat on his horse looking into the setting suns, back toward the Ridge, somewhere out there on the horizon, he began to feel it too; a creeping sense of premonition was settling in, a sense of pending doom, of a simple mission going vastly awry. He could feel it, sitting like a pit in his stomach.

And somehow, he, too, felt that they would never make it back again.

CHAPTER SEVENTEEN

Darius stood in the small circular courtyard, framed by tall stone walls, and faced the mysterious man opposite him, wondering. This trainer for the Empire, this man who had intervened and saved his life, stood there now, in his simple brown robe, with his simple staff, and Darius did not know what to make of him. Deklan, he had introduced himself as. On the one hand, he had saved his life, and for that, Darius felt eternally grateful; on the other hand, Darius had no idea why the man had went out of his way for him, or what he wanted. Would he turn out to be cruel, like all the others?

Deklan looked back at Darius and studied him as if he knew him. He looked upon Darius with respect, viewing him as a warrior would, and Darius did not understand why. This man, too, was so mysterious, so out of place here in the Empire, with his brown cloak and simple staff. Darius had never witnessed a man fight like that, take down so many soldiers with such a simple weapon. He was the most nimble fighter Darius had ever seen, and he sensed he could learn much from him.

Deklan stood there, so calm, staring back, as if waiting for something in the silence, and Darius did not know what to say or do. After all, this man clearly served the Empire—and that meant he would either be preparing to kill Darius himself, or preparing Darius for the arena—both of which amounted to the same thing: death.

As Darius watched, wary, the man stepped forward and removed a small ring of keys from his belt. To Darius's surprise, he unlocked each of his shackles. Immediately the heavy shackles fell to the ground, and Darius, feeling a million pounds lighter, rubbed his wrists and ankles, not realizing how much they had been weighing him down.

Deklan then surprised Darius further by drawing a sharpened sword from his belt, and reaching out and handing it to Darius, hilt first.

Darius stared down at it, unsure if it was a trick.

"Why would you give me a sword?" Darius asked. "I could kill you with it."

Deklan only smiled.

"You won't," he replied.

Darius looked down, staring at it, then slowly reached out and grabbed its hilt; it felt great to wield a sword again.

"You unlocked my shackles," Darius said. "Why?"

Deklan smiled back.

"You have nothing to fear from me," the man said. "It is far more dangerous for you outside these walls than inside them. All of my fellow soldiers would gladly kill you, while I am the only one who wants to keep you alive."

"But why?" Darius demanded.

Deklan moved a few feet away from Darius and studied him.

"It is my task to train these boys to fight in the arena. Not one has ever survived. I prolong their lives, yet I do not save them. Yet in you, I recognize something different. A boy who can, perhaps, survive."

Darius looked back skeptically.

"I recognize in you," he continued, "a boy who is also a man, and who deserves a chance to fight. A boy with a warrior's spirit should not be killed in a courtyard, with shackles and chains on him."

"So then you preserved my life only to make me a better fighter, so that those in the arena can have more enjoyment in watching my death?" Darius asked, annoyed.

Darius, disgusted, threw the sword down to the ground and it landed in the dirt with a clang and a small cloud of dust. He stared back at the man defiantly.

Deklan, surprised, shook his head slowly, then turned his back and circled the courtyard.

"Whether you lose your life quickly or go down fighting is your decision," he continued. "I offer to give you a chance. One chance. And that is the greatest gift I can give you. Enough talking," he said, facing him.

Darius stared back, looking down at the sword in the dirt, debating.

"If I kill you," Darius said, "you will be unable to train these boys. They will die sooner, the games will not be as exciting—and perhaps the Empire will end them altogether."

Deklan smiled.

"If only the Empire were that kind," he replied. "Death fulfills them, whether it is quick or slow. I am an insignificant cog in a machine far greater than us both. But if you believe I am the enemy, then let it out on me. Fight me. Come here and learn how to really fight. Unless you are afraid."

Darius burned with indignation, and he stepped forward, rubbing his wrists from the shackle marks, and reached down and took up the sword.

He studied its sharpened blade, and looked back at the man holding a simple staff.

"I have a blade of steel," Darius said, "and I have killed greater men than you. You have but a stick. It is not I who should fear."

Deklan smiled.

"Then see if that sharp blade of yours can damage my little stick. Unless you do not know how to wield it?"

Darius shouted out in a burst of rage and charged the man, thrilled to finally have a chance to let out all of his pent-up rage at someone.

Darius charged, raised the sword high, and brought it down on the man, who stood there perfectly still, with all his might.

Darius was surprised to find himself go stumbling past, as the man, with lightning quick speed, sidestepped him at the last moment.

Darius wheeled and faced him again, furious. He shouted and charged again.

This time, Deklan surprised him by not backing away or sidestepping—but rather stepping forward to meet him. As he did so, Deklan raised his staff sideways with both hands, and came in so close that he caught Darius's wrists as he was bringing the sword down, smashing them with the staff and causing Darius to drop his sword.

Darius hurriedly bent down to pick it up, but as he did, the man jabbed him with his staff in the chest, knocking him back on his butt.

Darius lay on the ground, humiliated, looking up at the man—who smiled and circled back across the courtyard before facing him again.

"Do you know the difference between a knight and a master warrior?" Deklan asked.

"A knight is gallant and proud and chivalrous; he is honorable and fearless. He charges into battle at a moment's notice, and he exhibits grace. He does not succumb to his fears."

Darius lunged for his sword, trying to retrieve it off the ground, thinking he might catch Deklan off guard; but Deklan saw it coming, and he waited until the last moment then struck it with his staff, knocking it out of Darius's reach. He then shoved Darius with his foot in his ribs, sending him rolling.

Deklan smiled down, unfazed.

"A master warrior, on the other hand," he continued calmly, "is all those things and more. He is the very first one into battle—or sometimes he is the last. He is not predictable, as the others; he has his own code. He has internalized the laws of battle and has made them his own—and morphed them to his own code. His primary objective is, always, to win.

"You can always sense a master warrior: he is very still. He need wield but a single, simple weapon. He needs to prove nothing to anyone. He might even appear motionless—but when the time comes, he will strike, in the most unexpected way, like lightning. Like a fly across the lake. Quick and fast and silent, you will never even be sure he was there. And with the slightest touch of his was weapon, he can do more damage than an entire legion of knights."

Darius, enraged, jumped to his feet, raced across the courtyard, grabbed the sword, and turned to charge Deklan—but as soon as he turned around, he was surprised to find Deklan right behind him, swinging his staff and sweeping his legs out from under him—sending him landing on his back on the desert floor.

"Your problem," Deklan continued calmly, standing over him, "is that you are still merely a knight. This arena is littered with the bodies of dead knights. I have trained them all. It is the home of the brave, a joust of knights. The path of the knight is to joust, to compete, to prove himself at all times. Most of all, to better himself. And what is needed to survive here is not merely a knight, but a warrior. A *master* warrior."

"And how would you know what is needed to survive, if no one ever has?" Darius asked, still in a fury, wiping blood from his lips as he jumped to his feet and raised the sword. He charged and quickly slashed downwards—but Deklan this time turned his staff sideways and deflected the sharp end of the blade. As Darius slashed, pushing Deklan back, Deklan deflected the blows, left and right, left and right, the sword clacking on the staff but never damaging it.

Deklan never broke a sweat, keeping his balance and his calm until had enough—he then reached around and spun his long staff sideways and smashed Darius's wrist, sending his sword flying through the air. In the same motion he spun the staff and smashed Darius in the side of the head, sending him stumbling down to the ground.

Darius, breathing hard, beaten, feeling more insecure than he'd ever had, finally realized the futility of fighting this man, who was a thousand times faster, quicker, stronger, and more deadly than he could ever be. He looked up into the sun as Deklan stood over him, holding out a hand.

Darius took it and let him pull him to his feet.

"I know," Deklan continued, "because I was the arena's sole survivor."

Darius stared back, flabbergasted.

"*You!?*" he asked. "*You* survived?"

Deklan said nothing, and Darius felt the mystery deepen about this man.

"Can you train me?" Darius asked, breathing hard, hopeful. "Can you train me to become a master warrior?"

Deklan surprised Darius by suddenly turning his back and walking away.

"I can point the way," he said. "But no one can teach you that but yourself."

As Darius watched the man go, he was suddenly filled with a burning curiosity.

"Who are you?" Darius shouted out after him.

But the man turned and exited through an iron door, leaving Darius alone in the courtyard, listening only to the sound of his own voice echoing back to him—and wondering why this mysterious man, whom he had just met, seemed so eerily familiar.

CHAPTER EIGHTEEN

Loti woke to the sound of slamming metal, and she jumped up and looked all around, wondering where she was. Her throat was parched and her eyes had a hard time adjusting in the dim light as she tried to shake the dreams from her mind. She had been dreaming of a never-ending journey, dreaming of riding an iron carriage off the face of the earth, falling off cliffs and landing somewhere in the ocean.

Loti woke on high alert, looking all around, trying to remember. It was stifling in here, hard to breathe, dust swirling in the air, and she looked all about and saw that she was encased by iron bars. She was in a cage, so low to the ground that she slammed her head as she tried to stand—and immediately knelt back down. She looked around and saw a dozen other bodies lying listlessly on the dirt floor. She turned and saw, beyond the cell bars, the dusty desert, waves of heat rippling off of it; she saw that she was in the center of a small, busy village, horses and carriages racing back and forth, slaves shackled and being paraded everywhere. She heard a sound, and her heart filled with dread to realize it was one she recognized all too well: a taskmaster stood close by, lashing a slave across the back.

Then she remembered: her mother. She had set her and her brother up, had sold them as slaves to this caravan. It was an act which she would never forgive.

"Sister," came a voice.

Loti's heart soared as she recognized it and turned to see her brother Loc, bound in shackles beside her. Her eyes filled with tears of relief.

They embraced, and she hugged him tight.

"You have been sleeping the entire day," he said. "The slave traders brought us here the night before and threw us in this cattle pen. Now we await our fate."

Loti was horrified as the reality of what their mother had done sank in.

"How could she do this to us?" she asked.

Loc sadly shook his head.

"She must have some reason," he said. "She must have thought it was best for us."

Loti shook her head in outrage; Loc had always stood up for their mother, regardless of what she had done.

"Better for us?" she asked. "How could this possibly be better than anything? We are slaves again."

He shrugged.

"Perhaps she thought that if we stayed with Darius, our fates would be worse."

There came a clanging of keys, and Loti turned and watched with horror as a taskmaster yanked out several slaves from the holding cell, grabbing them by their ankles and dragging them across the hard desert floor. With a kick and a shove, the shackled slaves were sent off to the fields of labor—joining hundreds of others who were chipping away at rock.

Two more taskmasters approached their cell, and Loti, burning with fury, reached down felt the dagger hidden in her waist. She would not succumb to a life as a slave—never again. This time she would go down fighting.

As the taskmasters approached, she turned to Loc.

"Not this time," she said with steely determination. "I shall never be a slave again."

Loc reached out and placed a reassuring hand on her wrist and shook his head in the darkness.

"Please, my sister. Don't do it. I beg you. For me. Save your fight for another time. You will kill one of them, and you will die."

"I will die anyway," she said. "And at least I shall kill one of them. Why should I not?"

"Because," he said quickly, urgently, "I want to kill *many* of them."

She looked at him, surprised by his response and by the deadly seriousness in his eyes. Slowly, she released her grip and slipped the dagger back into her waist.

"How?" she asked.

The taskmasters arrived at the cell, unlocking it, and as they reached to extract another slave, this time Loc rushed forward.

"We wish to volunteer!" he called out.

There came a stunned silence, as the taskmasters looked him over disparagingly.

"You?" one asked, laughing, mocking him.

Loc flushed.

"Do not pay attention to my hand," he replied. "I can mine as well as any man. I've been mining my entire life."

"What are you doing?" Loti whispered to him—but he ignored her.

"Mining!?" the taskmaster asked. "You know it is a job from which most slaves never return. No one volunteers for it. Nine out of ten will not come back."

Loc nodded.

"I know," he replied. "And I volunteer."

The taskmasters looked at each other, then one finally nodded to the other, and they pulled out Loti and Loc.

"What have you done?" Loti asked him, as they were led off.

He smiled back, a furtive smile that only she could see.

"You will see, my sister," he replied. "You will see."

CHAPTER NINETEEN

Erec stood in the village center, one arm hooked around Alistair's waist, and smiled wide as he relaxed for the first time and allowed himself to enjoy the festivities taking place all around him. He took a sense of pride in seeing these Empire villagers free from the grips of the Empire, all of them so jubilant, dancing and cheering all around him, such expressions of joy and laughter, the likes of which he had not seen in years. These people had been oppressed and enslaved for so long—he could see it in their faces—and now he had granted them the greatest gift: freedom.

Music rang in the air, and they played drums and smashed cymbals as they danced, each grabbing the other, locking arms, dancing in circles. Erec soon felt a villager grab him, a tall muscular man with no shirt, linking arms with him and dancing around in a circle. Erec found himself caught up in it all, laughing as he joined in, while a woman linked arms with Alistair and danced with her. Erec felt himself passed off from one partner to another as he let his guard down and enjoyed himself. He noticed all of his soldiers looking to him, to see if it was okay to join in, and as he nodded back, they all, too, relaxed and joined. Erec spotted his brother dancing beside him, and he felt his men all deserved a break, and a chance to celebrate their string of victories.

Oppression was a terrible thing, Erec knew, and having one's freedom stripped was perhaps the worst form of oppression there was. Freedom, the ability to master one's own destiny, was more than just precious—it was the essence of life itself. These people, now free, no longer feared danger, even though they lived in a land surrounded by Empire; they were free for *this moment*, and this moment was all that mattered. Whether they died later or not, this moment made their lives worth it.

As Erec took a break from dancing, though, he glanced back at his fleet, anchored in the river beside this village, and he felt a flash of concern: far off in the distance, in the black of night, he could still see the flames of those burning ships, lit up against the night, a soft glow of orange. Erec knew that was a good sign—the Empire was still struggling with their blockade. But he did not know how long it would last, and he felt a responsibility to keep moving.

As the latest song died down, Erec pulled aside the village chief, clasped him on the shoulder, and looked him in the eye.

"We are most grateful for your hospitality," Erec said.

"It is we who must thank you," the chief said. "How can we repay you? It is very sacred for our culture."

Erec shook his head.

"Seeing your joy is repayment enough," he said. Erec sighed. "I hate to say goodbye, but we must leave you now. I fear if we do not move on, the Empire shall catch up with us."

The chief's face showed no concern.

"You have nothing to worry about this night, my friend," he replied. "Empire soldiers would never travel these waters at night. They will wait for morning to pursue you."

Erec looked back, puzzled.

"Why?" he asked.

"The snakes," the chief replied. "Out there, in those black waters, there are monster snakes, the size of a ship, that surface at night. If they sense the motion of ships, they would drag them down."

Erec turned and examined the blackened waters with a new respect; he saw no snakes, but he took the chief at his word. The wonders of these Empire lands never ceased to amaze him.

"Stay this night with us," the chief added. "You will do us a great honor. You will be safer here—and we want to thank you, to celebrate with you."

He reached out and put a drink in Erec's hand, took a drink in his own, and clinked cups with him.

Erec hesitated, then finally leaned back and they drank together. Erec felt the warm spirits going to his head, and for the first time in a while, he felt relaxed.

Two huge moons hung over them, illuminating the night, the smell of roasting food strong in the air, and all his men were happy and relaxed. He nodded back and smiled.

"We will wait, my friend. Tonight, we celebrate."

*

Erec walked with Alistair through the starlit night, the two holding hands, heading away from the noise and bustle of the village's ongoing celebrations, after hours of dancing and eating and drinking. Erec felt lightheaded, the strong alcohol going to his head, and as he held Alistair's hand, they moved through the brush, heading down towards the river. They had been in constant flux since they had departed the Southern Isles, and he wanted some time alone with her.

Erec took in the skies and saw the two huge moons had long since dropped, the sky now black and replaced with countless twinkling stars, yellow, red, and green, punctuating the night, providing almost as much light as the moons. It was the first time he and Alistair had been alone together in he did not know how long. As he reflected on their past, on how she had saved his life, he felt guilty that they had never had time to wed.

"Do not think that I have forgotten about our wedding," he said. "One day soon, I promise, it shall come."

Alistair smiled back at him.

"In my eyes, we are already wed," she said.

They walked in silence for some time, and he could sense her breathing shallow, could sense her tension, as if there was something she wanted to say.

And then finally, she broke her silence:

"After all, my lord," she said, "our child will need a legitimate father."

Erec stopped and did a double take at her words, wondering if he had heard her correctly.

"Child!?" he asked.

Alistair stopped, too, and faced him, smiling back at him with a look of such joy and surprise.

"We are with child," she said.

Erec felt a wave of ecstasy rush over him, and he reached out and embraced her, holding her tight, spinning her around, again and again, overflowing with joy.

"Are you certain?" he asked, looking down at her stomach, his heart was slamming his chest.

She nodded, her eyes filled with joy.

"Yes," she said. "I wanted to tell you for so long...but...the moment did not feel right."

Erec hugged her again, overjoyed, his mind swimming with a million thoughts. He going to have a child. It was hard to fathom. He had always imagined this day, but had never imagined it would come now, so soon. He thought of all the people he had lost, all the hardship they had suffered, and this good news, the idea of bringing new life into the world, made him feel restored again. As if hope could live on, no matter what.

"You don't know what this means to me," he finally said.

They continued walking until they reached the river's edge and they both stopped before it and looked out at the river, hundreds of yards wide, like a vast lake, its black waters glistening beneath the starlight.

"And do you sense if it's a boy or girl?" he asked.

She smiled, raising a hand and feeling her stomach.

Finally she responded.

"I feel it's a girl, my lord."

The second she uttered the words, he felt they were true. He smiled wide, reached out and placed a hand on her stomach, thrilled. A boy or a girl—he was equally happy either way.

"I only wish we were not bringing her into such a world, filled with war and strife and subjugation from the Empire."

Alistair faced him.

"Perhaps it is up to us, my lord," she said, "to make our world free. To change the world she will enter before she does."

Erec felt the wisdom in her words.

There came a splashing in the river, and Erec turned and looked out and was shocked as he saw the outline of a huge snake, twenty feet long, rising up in the waters, only its body visible, a curve, rising from the surface then disappearing beneath it. He looked closely and saw the river was filled with the outlines of these huge snakes, splashing as they surfaced; the waters were teeming with them. He felt grateful not to be on board the ship, and realized the Empire the villagers had spared his life to keep him from the river at night.

Alistair tightened her grip on his hand, and he could feel her anxiety at being so close to the waters. He did not feel comfortable here either, so close to these monsters, and together, they turned and walked back toward the distant glow of the village and its revelries.

Erec was still spinning with the news, and he wanted to shout out, to share the news with everyone, he was so overjoyed. As they rejoined the festivities, though, the music slowly died down, and the villagers and Erec's people settled around the great bonfire in the center of the village, and Erec thought he would wait for a better time. He sat down beside Alistair, beside all the rest of them, and as they did, an old woman, with long, braided gray hair, down to her knees, sat in the center, her back to the fire, and looked out on all of them. She had the glowing, white eyes of a seer, and all soon fell silent as she commanded their attention.

The village chief, beside Erec, leaned over and explained.

"If she chooses to join us, as on this night, it is an honor. Sometimes she will say nothing at all; other times, on holy days or special days, such as today, she will choose to speak."

As the drums quieted to a slow and steady beat, the seer slowly turned, looking all about the circle, until she finally settled her gaze on Alistair. She raised a finger, pointing at her.

"Your child," she began.

Erec felt his heart beating as he saw the woman pointing at Alistair's stomach, amazed that she knew. He was both eager and afraid to hear what the seer had to say.

"She will conquer kingdoms," the seer continued. "She will be powerful, more powerful than you both combined. She has a great destiny. A special destiny. And her destiny will be linked with one other's….You have a brother," she said. "And he has a son. Guwayne. Your daughter's destiny shall be linked to Guwayne's."

Alistair stared back, clearly shocked.

"How?" Alistair asked.

But the woman closed her eyes and turned away. Soon, the drumbeats became louder, and it was clear that her visions were done for the night.

Erec was baffled as he contemplated her words. He was of course proud to father such a powerful child, and yet he did not understand what it all meant. He looked at Alistair and could see her confusion, too.

"Tomorrow, when you depart from this place, you will have a choice," said a voice.

Erec turned to see the village chief beside him, his men gathered around, staring back at him earnestly, concern on his face.

"As you travel upriver, it will fork," he continued. "The eastern fork will lead you to Volusia, to your people. The western fork leads to a powerful Empire outpost, in our beloved sister village. In it are hundreds of our people, captives to the Empire, needing freedom, as we. If you free them, they will come to us, and we will be twice as strong, a growing army. If you do not, the outpost will soon arrive here and kill us. We are no match for their armor or weaponry. Our fate lies in your hands. I cannot expect you to help us anymore. If the freedom you granted us is just for this night, then even for this, we are grateful."

Erec stood there, looking out into the night, and he could feel all eyes locked on him. Yet again, he faced a difficult choice. It would, he knew, be a long and sleepless night.

CHAPTER TWENTY

Godfrey sat beside Akorth, Fulton, Ario, and Merek, hunched over a bar in the back alleys of Volusia, and nursing his woes over a series of drinks. He took another long sip of ale, foam dripping over the sides of the mug, and once again he admired this Empire beer. It was strong, dark brown, with a nutty flavor, and it was so smooth going down his throat. He had never tasted anything like it, and he was sure he never would again. It was reason enough to stay in Volusia.

He finished it, his fifth in a row, and motioned to the bartender for another. Two more appeared before him.

"Don't you think you should slow down just a touch?" came a voice.

Godfrey looked over to see Ario staring disapprovingly, the only one of their group without a drink, Akorth, Fulton and Merek already deep into theirs.

"I don't understand a man who does not drink," Godfrey said, "especially in times like this."

"And I don't understand a man who does," Ario countered, "especially you. You vowed not to drink again."

Godfrey belched, feeling disappointed with himself, knowing Ario was right.

"I thought I would save Darius," Godfrey said, despondent. "A lot of good that did."

Godfrey saw in his mind's eye Darius being swept away from the city, in that iron carriage, and once again, he beat himself up for it. He felt it was all his fault he did not reach him in time. Now, purposeless, he felt there was nothing to do but drown his sorrows.

"We *did* save him," Merek said. "If not for our poison, he would have been gored by that other elephant and mauled in the arena."

A dog barked and Godfrey looked down and saw Dray at his feet, and remembered he was there; Godfrey gave him more scraps of meat from the bar and a sip of his ale, and he felt good about himself for at least being able to take care of Darius's dog.

106

"We saved him for a short while only," Godfrey said, "only to be shipped off to an even crueler death."

"He might make it," Akorth said. "He's a tough one."

Godfrey looked down into his drink and he felt disgusted with himself. Saving Darius, as he had seen it, had been his chance to redeem himself. Losing him had put him into a deep depression, making him wonder what he had left to live for, what purpose he had in this life. He was supposed to help save Gwendolyn and the others; but now Gwendolyn was somewhere out there, lost in the Great Waste, probably dead, and all his people along with her. His infiltrating Volusia, as brave as it had seemed at the time, had turned out to be all for nothing.

Godfrey snapped out of it as he suddenly felt a strong hand clasp him on the shoulder and turned to see several Empire soldiers smiling back at him good-naturedly.

"Don't mind our squeezing in beside you, friend," one soldier said beside him.

At first, Godfrey was caught off guard by their familiarity—but then he remembered that he and the others were wearing the Empire armor that the Finian woman, Silis, had given them, and he realized the soldier thought they were one of them. It was a perfectly disguise, he had to admit, the armor fitting them all perfectly, and hard to distinguish races with the faceplates they wore, giving them room only to drink their drinks.

"Quite a bout today, wasn't that?" one of the soldiers asked him. "Were you at the arena? Did you see the boy win?"

"All too well," Godfrey grumbled, wanting them to disappear, in no mood to talk to anyone—especially these men.

"And what does that mean?" asked another soldier, an edge to his voice. "It was the greatest match of our time, the first time a Volusian won, would be shipped to represent us in the capital. You sound as if you take no pride in it."

Godfrey could hear the aggression rising in the drunk man's voice, and in the past he would have slinked away, avoided confrontation. But that was the old Godfrey. Not he was a man pushed too far, a man bitter at the world, with nothing left to lose.

"And why would I take pride in such a disgusting display of cruelty and barbarism?" Godfrey replied harshly, turning to the man.

The room fell silent, a heavy tension in the air, as the soldier squared off with him, and Godfrey felt all eyes on them. He gulped, wondering what he'd gotten himself into.

"A soldier who doesn't like the arena," the soldier said, examining Godfrey with a growing curiosity. "That is no soldier at all. What division do you hail from anyway?" he asked, looking his armor up and down.

Again, Godfrey could have invented a lie, as he might have in the past, and diffused the situation; but something in himself would not allow him to. He was done hiding from people, done backing down. He felt something growing strong within him, the blood of his father, perhaps, the blood of a long line of kings coursing through his veins. The time had finally come, he felt, to stand up for himself, regardless of the consequences.

He felt Merek's, Akorth's and Fulton's cautionary hands on his shoulder, willing him to back down, but he shrugged them off.

"I hail from no division," Godfrey boomed back, standing straighter. "I am not of the Empire at all. I am man in disguise, whose goal is to save my friends from the arena, to sabotage your army, to sabotage this city and to destroy all of you."

The room fell dead silent, as all the soldiers stared back at him, mouths agape, in shock.

The silence went on for so long, Godfrey thought it would never end, bracing himself for the dagger in his heart that would inevitably come.

But instead, to his shock, the soldier facing him suddenly boomed out with laughter. All around him, the other soldiers burst into laughter, too.

The soldier clasped Godfrey's shoulder.

"That was a good one," he said. "Very, very good. For a moment I thought you were telling the truth."

Godfrey slowly removed his helmet, revealing his human face, his hair, slick with sweat, sticking to his forehead, and he smiled back at them all.

Slowly, the Empire faces around the room fell in shock.

"This is for Darius," he said.

Godfrey squeezed tight the handle of his mug, stepped forward, swung it down and smashed the soldier over the head, sending him stumbling back and down to the ground.

Godfrey stood there, hardly believing what he had just done, looking back at all the hostile faces and knowing that in moments, he would be dead. But for this moment, at least, he was victorious, and no one, and nothing, would ever take that away from him.

CHAPTER TWENTY ONE

Thorgrin stood on the stern of the ship, looking up at the skies and watching Lycoples fly off into the horizon, screeching, flapping her wings, on the way to some distant world to bring his message to Gwendolyn. Thor wondered as he watched her fly away. Would Lycoples ever find her? If so, would she be able to help her? To save her from whatever trouble she was? To help reunite the two of them?

Or was it all already too late? Was Gwendolyn—Thor flinched to think of it—already dead?

It broke Thor's heart, watching Lycoples go. He felt a longing to be back up in the sky, on the back of a dragon, racing through the clouds. Being up there made him feel invincible, as though he could crisscross the world, as though anything could be his.

Thor turned back and looked ahead, at the waterfall of blood looming before them, raining down red, the noise growing increasingly louder. As they drifted toward it, the waters threatening to engulf their ship, already staining the masts red from the splashing, the others beside him—Reece, Selese, Indra, Elden, O'Connor, Matus, and Angel—all looked to him for guidance. Thor stared at the raging waters dropping from the sky, their sound deafening, with a sense of foreboding. He had never seen anything quite like this, and as he looked at the force of the wall of water, he had a sinking feeling the force of it might crush their ship. And yet he knew that his son lay beyond that wall—and that was all that mattered to him now. Nothing could hold him back.

"Thorgrin?" Reece asked, standing beside him, wanting to know what was on everyone's minds. "Do we turn back?"

Thor took a deep breath, then finally shook his head.

"We sail forward," he said. "Through the waterfall. Whatever the costs. Are you with me?" he asked the others, knowing it had to be their decision, too.

All of them, without hesitation, nodded back—and Thor felt more grateful for their loyalty than ever.

"Raise the sails!" Thor called out. "And angle them. We shall use them to deflect the waters!"

They all rushed into action, Thor jumping in and helping, and he felt his anxiety rising as the waves all around them grew choppier, the noise from the falls becoming deafening. The deck was becoming slick with blood, as the spray covered it, and Thor found himself slipping, along with the others.

Angel cried out as she went sliding right past Thor, heading for the rail, flailing, unable to stop herself—and Thor reached out and grabbed her arm just in time, saving her.

They all worked the sails, and Thor noticed the ship going adrift, turning sideways into the falls. He knew it would be deadly if they didn't enter at the right angle.

"OARS!" Thor called out.

They all rushed to grab oars, and Thor, too, grabbed an oar and began to row with all his might. The ship began to straighten again, sailing directly into the wall of blood, the current sucking them in. The sails above bent and curved beneath the weight of the spray, deflecting much of it into the sea, but not enough to keep the decks from beginning to fill.

They sailed closer and closer, nearly entering the waters, and as they did, Thorgrin felt small hands clutching his leg.

"I'm scared," Angel said, standing beside him.

Thor laid a reassuring hand on her head.

"Do not fear," he said. "Stay close to me, no matter what. I shall protect you."

"Do you promise?" she asked.

Thor looked down at her meaningfully.

"I vow," he shouted, over the din. "With all my life."

Angel clutched Thor's leg tighter, and Thor grabbed onto the rail, slick with blood.

"Under the sails, all of you!" Thor called out.

They all followed him under the sails, shielding them from the force of the rain.

"Grab onto anything you can!" he yelled, as he grabbed a rail tight, steadying himself, and each of the others grabbed the mast, a post—anything they could hold onto as they entered the falls.

A moment later, Thorgrin raised his hands above his head and heard the shouts of the others, as they were all immersed in a world of red. A wall of blood rained down on them, louder and more powerful than any falls he had seen, and their boat rocked violently, the waters churning, bobbing up and down, rocking left and right. Thor heard the ship groaning in protest, and for a moment he felt certain that they would not survive.

Thor felt blood soaking his hair, his eyes, his entire body; he wiped it away constantly, and yet still it was hard to see, hard to breathe. It was like buckets of thick water being dumped on his head.

Thor felt Angel clutching him tighter, beginning to slide across the deck. He reached down and grabbed her, too, and held her tight. With his other hand he held the mast, but everything was now slick with blood, and it was getting harder to hold on to anything.

The waves grew rougher, the ship jerking in every direction, and Thorgrin felt as if they would all be sucked down to a horrible death. He could barely hold on, and as he heard a shout, he looked up and watched O'Connor lose his grip and begin to slide across the deck, the ship now sideways, and about to hurl into the sea. There was no way he could reach him in time.

Suddenly, they burst through the falls. The world of red opened up to a world of night, and the ship straightened out as the waterfalls lightened. The deafening sounds receded, and as they sailed farther away, they found themselves on the other side of the wall, the heavy downpour of the waters replaced with a spray. The world was becoming quiet again, the waves calming, and Thor took stock: he saw all the others, dripping with blood, all in shock, as he—but all alive.

He turned back and looked over his shoulder and was shocked to see the strength of the falls they had just passed through. Their strength looked great enough to cut a man in half, and he did not know how they had survived.

The ship groaned, and Thor looked up to see the mast cracked in half, and looked about to see the damage the ship had taken; it had been badly beaten up, and yet still it sailed. Thor took a step and heard his feet splashing, and he looked down and saw the deck was filled with a good two feet of blood. At least, though, they had not capsized.

Thor saw the ship threatening to list, and he knew if they did not bail it soon, it could sink.

"Pails!" Thor yelled, and they all rushed into action. One at a time they each scooped up the water, even Angel joining in, and dumped bucket after bucket of blood overboard.

They worked diligently and soon enough the decks were mostly clear, save for a thin layer of blood, and the ship began to balance itself again.

Finally safe, Thor walked to the bow and took a moment to look out at the sight. He was in awe. Before them lay a whole new world, a vista unlike anything he had ever seen. The sea here was made of blood, viscous, their ship moving more slowly in it, like sailing through seaweed. In the waters he could see strange red fish, their fins transparent, rising and submerging beneath the water. There were other creatures, too, strange species he did not recognize; an octopus-like creature raised its head above the water, only to plunge back down beneath the surface again. Thor heard a great splashing and turned to the side to see a huge, red whale-like creature surfacing, with four heads and two long tails, blowing its spout before disappearing back beneath the waters.

Angel look up at him, in shock.

"Are we safe here?" she asked.

Thor nodding reassuringly.

"We are safe," he replied, not so sure himself.

Slowly, she released her grip on his leg.

On the horizon, Thor saw the outline of land on all sides of them, shaped in a horseshoe, a horizon of black, faint, distant. It seemed so far away. The land here seemed to be made of black, charred soil, perhaps even sulfur or tar, with streaks of glowing red in it, as if the gates of hell had opened and oozed onto them.

"The land oozes blood," Reece observed, coming up beside him.

"Perhaps we should make land," Elden said.

Indra shook her head.

"That is not land," she said. "What you see is merely the outskirts of the Land of Blood. That is boiling tar and lava. If we set foot on it, it would scald us. We must stick to the oceans, see where it brings us."

Thor looked up at the sky, dark and smoldering, threatening, ominous; it was a sky with no life in it, a sky filled with ash and streaked with scarlet. It was a land of gloom, the gloomiest place Thor had ever been. It was day here, but it felt like night.

Thor could sense the evil hanging heavy in this land, and he felt a foreboding as he thought of Guwayne, brought here by those creatures. What plan did they have in store for him?

*

Thorgrin stood quietly at the rail of the ship, looking out at the bleak landscape and wiping the blood off the rail with a soaked rag. All around him, the others did the same. A peaceful air had finally fallen over them, and now they were all trying to pick up the pieces, to clean up the mess and restore order. High above, the mast groaned as O'Connor and Elden finally finished fastening it back into place. The sails flapped overhead, stained red with blood, as Reece and Angel scrubbed them, trying to get them white again. Of course, the aesthetics didn't matter—but it was symbolic. They all wanted to prove to themselves that they were not crushed.

The sails were at full mast as they tacked and caught a strong wind, sailing deeper and deeper in the silence into this red sea, heading inevitably toward a sky of darkness and blood. Thor craned his neck and looked up at the sky and felt as if he were embraced by a world of gloom—a world that had no end. They had finally reached a period of calm and stillness, and as Thor looked up at the skies he wondered if it was afternoon, evening, or night. He could not tell in this place. The skies appeared to be filled with ash, streaked with scarlet, with no change to them. It was like a permanent state of twilight.

"How long until we get there?" came a voice.

Thor looked over to Angel standing beside him, wringing out a cloth over the edge. Then he looked out at the horizon, wondering the same thing himself.

"I wish I knew," he answered.

Thor heard the gentle lapping of the waters and he looked down at the red sea, the waters so thick that it slowed their ship, despite the breeze. The sea was eerily still, punctuated every now and again by the splashing of a strange creature that surfaced then disappeared just as quickly.

Thor searched the horizon, burning with a desire to find his son, and having a sinking feeling that he was losing him. He knew the ship was going as fast as its sails could take them and that there wasn't much else he could do.

Thor looked at the others and saw how exhausted they all were from the trip through the waterfalls, from the constant searching for

Guwayne. He felt bad that he had dragged them into this yet he also knew they were his brothers and sisters and that they would not take no for an option. He knew that if the roles were switched, he would do the same for them; he would, in fact, gladly give up his life for any one of them.

Thor saw Angel suddenly slump down, her back against the mast, and sit there, her eyes heavy, closing and then opening them again as she wiped her brow with the back of her hand.

Thor hurried and knelt beside her.

"What's wrong?" he asked, filled with concern.

She closed her eyes and nodded, looking exhausted.

"I'm sorry," she said. "It's just…been getting worse lately."

There studied her.

"What is?" he asked.

Listlessly, she raised her arm, white and covered in bumps from the leprosy.

"My sickness," she said. "It's been getting worse lately. It's spreading. Sometimes I feel well, but other times…I don't feel myself so much."

Thor felt awful, helpless. He leaned in and gave her a kiss on her forehead.

"What can I do?" he asked.

She smiled sweetly at him and grabbed his hand.

"Sit with me," she said.

Thor sat beside her, and the others came over and sat beside them, too.

"Isn't there anything we can do?" Selese asked.

Angel shook her head.

"I had a friend, on the island, who had it as bad as me," she said. "When she reached my age, she got sicker. It took her about six months."

Thor stared back with concern.

"Six months for what?" he asked.

She looked at him, terror and sadness in her eyes.

"Until she died," she answered flatly.

Thor's heart broke.

"It's okay," she said to him, smiling through tear-filled eyes, laying a hand on his wrist. "I always knew I was going to die. I just

115

never knew that I was going to live—to *really* live. You've given that to me. And I can never thank you enough."

Thor felt determined.

"I will *not* let you die," he insisted. He reached over and grabbed her hand. "Do you understand me? Whatever I have to do, whatever it takes, I will not let you die."

She wiped away a tear.

"I believe that if you could, you would," she said. "But you are not God. And Selese, even with all her powers, has tried to heal me, and even she cannot. Neither could Alistair." She shook her head sadly. "Not everyone is meant to be on this world forever."

Thor felt his heart tearing up inside.

"There must be a cure," he said. "Is there not *some* cure!?" he demanded.

Angel looked off into the distance, her eyes glassy.

"On the island, they all talked, all the time, of a cure," she said. "Some swear one exists. Others think it's just a fantasy of the desperate few. Whether it really exists…I don't know."

"What is it?" Thor pressed, determined. "Where is it?"

She shook her head.

"I know not what it is," she replied. "As far as where….well, some claim it lies between the Western Horns of the Empire. In the Land of the Giants."

Thor and all the others exchanged a curious look.

"The Land of the Giants?" Selese asked.

Angel nodded, her eyes heavy.

Thor turned to Indra, the expert on all things Empire.

"Do you know it?" he asked her.

Indra nodded grimly.

"I've heard of it," she said. "A place of terror. They are a fierce nation, answering to no one—not even the Empire. All who venture there do not return."

Thor felt filled with resolve, felt it burning in his stomach. He turned to Angel.

"Then that is where we shall go," he said. "We will rescue Guwayne, then we will find you your cure."

Angel slowly shook her head, smiling.

"You are very sweet to care about me," she replied. "But it would be in vain. It might not even exist—and you would all die trying."

Thor looked at the others, and they all looked back at him, equally resolved.

"Then all of us shall die," Reece chimed in, all of the others nodding.

Angel looked around the circle, and Thor detected new hope in her eyes.

Thor clutched Angel's hand, white with leprosy, and held on tight. He was determined to follow through on his word: he would find a way to cure her, whatever it took.

They continued to sail deeper into the ocean of blood, a comfortable silence settling over them, punctuated by the howl of the wind and the splashing of exotic fish alongside the boat. The gloom settled over all of them, matching Thorgrin's mood. There was something about this place that he sensed, something he did not like or trust, which he felt sinking deeper and deeper into him. It was like there was a depression that swirled in the air, and that sunk into his being the longer he was here. As much as he tried to block them out, Ragon's final words rang through his head: Even with all your powers…you would surely die if you go there. *All* of you would. Had he been right? Was broaching that waterfall, entering the Land of Blood, a feat too great for even him? Was he setting himself up for failure and death—and all his friends along with him?

He had no choice but to find out. Guwayne was out there on that horizon, somewhere, and as long as he was, turning around was not an option.

With full sails and land still far off, there was little for them to do. In the long silence, Reece sat there, holding Selese, who leaned back in his arms; Elden sat beside Indra, trying to drape an arm over her shoulder, which she reluctantly allowed; O'Connor polished his bow and Matus his flail—while Thor held the Sword of the Dead in his hands, examining all the fine detail on its ancient and mysterious hilt, brow furrowed as he thought of Guwayne. Was he safe now? Thor wondered.

Reece, sitting beside Thorgrin, cleared his throat.

"Old friend," he said to Thor, who looked up at him. "You and I have been on many quests together—more than I can count—and

117

I've rarely seen you so concerned as you are now. But you must let it go, so your mind is clear for the battle ahead. I know you worry for Angel. We all do. But if this cure exists, we shall find it. And as far as your Guwayne…whatever it takes, we shall find him too. We are with you."

Thor was overwhelmed with gratitude for his friend's support.

"You are right, my friend," Thor replied. "A warrior's mind must always be clear."

Reece sighed.

"When I was young," Reece continued, after a long while, "all I wanted was to be a member of the Legion. I wanted it so badly, I could taste it. I would stay up all night, night after night, pining for it. I imagined myself in the armor, imagined myself wielding its weapons…. But my father, the King, told me I could not join—unless I earned it."

Thor looked back at his friend in wonder; he had never heard this story before.

"But I always assumed you were just given a position in the Legion," Thor replied. "After all, you are the son of a King."

Reece shook his head.

"That is why I was not," Reece replied. "He wanted me to earn it, like everybody else—but more than that, he demanded I excel, beyond a normal Legion member. The trials I was given were twice as hard as the others. Nothing I did was ever good enough for him."

Reece sighed.

"I resented it at the time, and I hated my father. I could understand equality—but what he put me through was unjust. At the time, I viewed him as a tyrant, intent on keeping me from when I wanted most."

Reece looked out at the horizon long time, clearly thinking.

"And now?" Thor finally asked, curious.

"And now," Reece finally continued, "looking back, I understand why he did what he did. Now I finally realize that he was not training me for the Legion: he was training me for life. He *wanted* me to experience something unfair, because *life* can be unfair. He wanted me to excel and rise above what was merely necessary, because in life, often we need to excel beyond what is needed from us. He wanted me to experience adversity and perseverance because it is often through

118

them that we reach our goals. And he wanted to withhold for me what I wanted most in life because he wanted me, above all, to fight for it.

"Above all," Reece continued, "he wanted me to achieve it on my own because, if he had just given it to me, it would've been valueless to me. I would have resented him for it my whole life. As much as I hated him then, I love him for it now. It was something he didn't give me—and that, ironically, was the greatest gift of all."

Reece looked at Thor meaningfully.

"That, after all," Reece continued, "is what it means to be a warrior. Nothing is given to him, nothing is handed to him. What is his, he takes, earns by his own hands, his own merit. Not by our fathers' hands, and not by our family name. But by our own name, by the name we are forced to forge for ourselves."

Thorgrin thought about what Reece said, and the words resonated with him more, than he knew.

"The world is filled with people telling us what we cannot achieve," Reece said. "It is up to us to prove them wrong."

Thorgrin, inspired, reached out and clasped Reece's forearm.

"We are brothers," he said. "And we shall be until the day we die."

"Brothers," Reece replied solemnly.

These men here, on this ship, Thor realized, were all brothers to him now, more so any family he'd ever had.

"Up ahead!" called a voice.

Thor jumped to his feet and ran to the bow as Indra stood there, pointing at something on the horizon. Thor looked out and saw the land mass on the horizon narrowing, the blackened shores and cliffs visible, and he saw that they were being funneled into a long channel, steep black cliffs on either side.

Indra gasped quietly.

Thor looked at her, concerned.

"What is it?" he asked.

Indra shook her head

"The Straits of Madness," she said, fear in her voice.

She turned and looked at the others, and for the first time, Thor saw hesitation in her face.

"It is a place no human must go. We must turn the ship around."

Thor looked straight ahead at the churning red waters, becoming more violent in the straits, the sharp cliffs framing it, and while at first he felt hesitation, he then remembered Reece's story. He knew he must forge on.

Thor grabbed the rail and held on, as others did the same.

"Shall we turn back?" Indra called out, panic in her voice.

Thor shook his head.

"We never turn back," he replied. "Never again!"

Everyone braced themselves as the ship caught the wind, and it took them right into the Straits of Madness, and into the jaws of a likely death.

CHAPTER TWENTY TWO

Darius stood at the entrance to the Capital arena, the roar deafening as he looked up at the thousands of Empire citizens in the coliseum, shaking the ground as they all screamed out for blood. Darius was chained to dozens of other gladiators, faces he did not even look at this time, faces he did not even want to recognize: he knew that soon they, like he, would all be dead.

Darius tried to drown out the noise, this arena so vast, so overwhelming, dwarfing the other arena in size. He had never seen anything like it—it was a spectacle beyond the imagination. So many people, he thought, so devoted to bloodshed and cruelty.

Standing beside him, in his brown robes, was Deklan, holding his staff and looking out serenely, as if he had seen it a thousand times before.

There came a roar of approval from the crowd, and Darius looked out. He tried not to look, but he couldn't help it: there, in the center of the arena, were dozens more gladiators, chained to each other, looking in every direction nervously. A horn sounded, and Empire soldiers, donning armor and wielding fine weaponry, attacked the defenseless gladiators.

It was a slaughter. Some tried to fight back bravely with the crude weapons they had been given, their swords blunted steel and practically useless. Those that survived were pushed backwards until they stumbled into giant pits which opened up in the floor. They cried out as they landed in sharpened spears, before the pits closed up again.

A horn sounded and the Empire soldiers fell to the ground—as they did, blades flew and spun through the air, decapitating any gladiators left alive.

The crowd roared in delight as another horn sounded and the Empire soldiers stood. Dozens of bloody corpses littered the stadium floor, and Empire servants rushed out and began to drag them away, cleaning the floor, preparing it for the next wave.

Darius felt a fresh wave of anxiety as he stood there. He knew he was up next.

Deklan turned to him.

"Forget everything you know," Deklan said urgently. "This arena is like nothing you're used to. The Empire fights neither clean nor fair. There is no common enemy: the enemy is on all sides of you. The dangers are everywhere. This is not an honorable match between two knights. This is a spectacle of death."

"And this is what you've trained me for?" Darius asked. "Then what was the point of it all?"

Deklan's face fell, and Darius sensed a break in his calm façade in a new look of sorrow.

"I wanted you to have a chance," he replied.

"A chance?" Darius repeated. "What chance could I possibly have?"

Deklan remained silent.

"You think you are better," Darius continued. "Better than them. Not of the Empire. But you *are* one of them. You think that if you train us, it puts you above them. You are still on their side, not ours. And when I die today, my blood will be on your hands, as much as any of theirs."

Deklan frowned.

"I have no choice," he replied. "I am held captive by them, just as you. I do not enjoy what I do. But at least I use whatever life I have to help keep you alive."

Darius shook his head.

"You are wrong," he replied. "You do have a choice. There is always a choice. It just depends on how much you want to sacrifice for it."

Darius looked meaningfully into this man's eyes and he sensed some great war going on inside him, some failed lifetime; he sensed a once-great and honorable warrior deep down inside. He wanted to appeal to the man's chivalry, his code of honor, and he felt that it was there—but just out of reach, suppressed just a bit too deep after all these years.

Deklan stared back, unable to respond, and Darius could see the haunted look in his eyes.

A horn sounded, the crowd erupted, and Darius felt himself shoved into the arena, shackled to all the other gladiators, squinting into the blazing sun as the crowd went wild. The earth shook beneath them as they went, prodded deeper and deeper into the arena.

Darius coughed at the great clouds of dust, and as he felt the heat of the two suns beating down on him, he clutched at the dinky little sword he had been given, its blade not sharp enough to even cut his own shackles. Finally, his group stopped in the middle, the crowd on its feet, and Darius looked all about with the others nervously, wondering from which direction danger would strike.

A low horn sounded, and Darius felt the hairs rise on his spine as he suddenly heard a horrific roar, one he did not recognize. The crowd cheered, as if familiar with it, and Darius knew this could not be good.

Darius was shocked as he saw concealed doors open on all sides of the arena, and animals that looked like pumas—except twice the size, with glowing yellow eyes—come running out toward them. The gladiators wheeled and looked in every direction, petrified.

They ran faster than anything Darius had ever seen, and one of them set its sights on Darius. It locked on him and ran right for him, snarling, preparing to pounce.

Darius braced himself as the animal leapt into the air, fangs extended for his throat. Darius raised his sword, but the creature merely swatted it from his grip.

It landed atop Darius, the first of the gladiators to be attacked, and the crowd roared as they wrestled down to the ground. The animal slashed his arm, drawing blood with its three sharp claws, and Darius shouted out in pain.

It then spun atop him and the beast opened its huge jaws to clamp down on his face.

Darius grabbed its throat, all muscle, barely holding it at bay as the beast dripped saliva onto his face. Hands shaking, Darius knew he had to move fast.

Darius finally managed to dodge to the side, and the beast's fangs went into the dirt. He then rolled around, grabbing it from behind, wrapped his arm around its neck, and twisted with all his might.

There came a crack—then the beast went limp in his arms. Dead.

The crowd roared, and all around Darius he heard the shouts of other gladiators, shouting as they fought off the animals, most of them dying and a few, like Darius, wrestling.

Darius sensed motion, saw another leap for him, and he rolled, grabbed his sword, held it high, and let the weight of the beast impale itself on it, falling right atop him, dead.

Darius pushed it off of him and rolled over, breathing hard, the pain from the scratches killing his arm, and he braced himself as more came bounding his way. Darius scrambled to his knees, his heart pounding, wondering what he was going to do as several more beasts ran for him at once. He looked side to side as he heard the moans, and noticed that already many gladiators were dead, the beasts standing on their chests, biting them.

Suddenly a horn sounded, and all the beasts, as suddenly as they had appeared, turned and ran off, disappeared back into the concealed doors all around the arena. At first, Darius breathed a deep sigh of relief—but then he realized: the Empire was only setting the stage for something far worse to come.

Darius suddenly heard a whistling noise cutting through the air, too loud, and coming way too fast. He couldn't figure out what it was, and when he turned, he could not believe the sight before him: metal chains swung through the air, suspended from the highest point of the arena, and at the end of them were immense spiked iron balls, nearly as large as Darius. There were dozens of these balls, suddenly swinging across the stadium, crisscrossing in every direction—and aimed right for the center of the arena.

"Look out!" Darius shouted to the gladiator beside him, shoving him out of the way while at the same time dropping down face-first to the ground.

As Darius hit the ground he looked up and watched the gladiator on the other side of him turn around to see what was happening—but too late. The metal ball smashed him, impaled him and continued to rise with him up on it, as the crowd cheered like crazy.

Darius kept his head low to the ground as the metal balls swung in every direction, impaling many of the gladiators, killing them on the spot. This arena, he realized, was vastly different from the one in Volusia: it was built for sport. It was cruel and unpredictable.

Merciless, lacking honor. At least in Volusia, others were brave enough to stand before him.

As the swinging chains and balls receded, finally another horn sounded, and as the chains were withdrawn, Darius found himself standing there, one of but a half-dozen gladiators left, facing the great iron doors in the center of the arena wall. Darius felt his heart pounding in anticipation, as a great groaning of metal filled the air and the doors slowly opened wide.

The crowd roared, standing to see as immense creatures were brought forth, shackled to each other, hulking one step at a time. They looked like humans, but were three times the size, standing perhaps twenty feet tall, broad, muscles bulging, with three huge eyes in their head, no nose, and a mouth made of jagged teeth. They walked with a sickening sound, and with each step they took, the crowd went crazy.

An Empire soldier rushed forward and cut their chains, and as he did, the creatures were let loose. They leaned back and roared, a sickening sound, and then set their sights on Darius and the others. Darius felt a chill run up his spine: he knew these would be the most formidable foes he'd ever met.

The creatures rushed forward, running faster than Darius could imagine, with huge strides, reaching them in no time. As one thundered down upon him wielding an immense battle-ax, Darius raised his sword and blocked. It was the most intense blow he had ever received, and it shook his body to its core, sending him to the ground and shattering his sword in two.

Darius saw stars as he lay there, looking side to side as heard the screams; he saw fellow gladiators being crushed by these creatures, battle-axes chopping them in half, and others being stampeded. These creatures were just too big, too fast, too powerful, to oppose.

As Darius blinked, in but a moment all the others lay dead. Darius was the only one left alive.

Darius rolled out of the way as an ax swept down for his head; it lodged in the ground beside him, just missing his head, and as Darius rolled out of the way, he used his chains to trip the creature.

The creature, caught off guard, landed on its back, its legs swept out from under it. The crowd roared, shocked by the development, clearly not expecting one of the creatures to fall.

Darius wasted no time: he rolled, raised his word high, and plunged it into the creature's throat as he lay prone, killing it.

The crowd jumped to its feet and went wild, its applause thunderous.

Darius, emboldened, breathing hard, gained his feet, snatching the creature's dropped sword, and faced the rest. It felt good to hold real steel.

Immediately another came at him with an ax. Darius suddenly recalled what Deklan had taught him: *stay calm, stay centered, be in the moment. Do not let your emotions cloud you.*

Darius, focused, waited until the right moment, then he ducked. The creature's ax swung sideways just over his head; as Darius ducked, he raised his new sword and sliced the creature's stomach, sending it to its knees. Dead.

The crowd again went wild.

Darius turned as more of these creatures charged him. Furious, they converged on him, roaring ferociously, their sharpened fangs showing. Darius did not back down, steeling himself for the confrontation, knowing he could do this, knowing he was stronger than he thought, however scary the foe.

As they reached him, Darius held his ground. He raised his sword and blocked the blows of the great axes, one after another after another, turning side to side, dodging and weaving, fending off the creatures. Exhausted, it was all he could do to just stay on his feet. But he didn't turn and run.

Finally one of them kicked him, and Darius went flying back. He landed flat on his stomach on the ground, losing his sword. He rolled and looked up at the sky, and as he did, he saw a hatchet coming down for his head.

It was too late. With nothing left to do, Darius braced himself to finally meet his end.

CHAPTER TWENTY THREE

Stara strolled through the gardens in the royal court of the Ridge, twisting her way through them, smelling the flowers but not really seeing them, so lost in thought, memories, and depression. Stara could not shake the past from her mind, could not shake images of Reece, of her love for him—of their love for each other. She kept reliving in her mind that last moment she had seen him, disembarking from Gwen's ship to join Thorgrin on his search for his son.

It tore her up inside. She had begged him not to go, but there had been little she could do to change his mind. It was infuriating and made her feel helpless at the same time.

Stara could not forget the argument they'd had the night before, in the hold of the ship, each trying to get away from the other, yet each unable to get away from one another. They blamed each other for Selese's death, and it tainted every glance they took.

Yet deep down, Stara knew that Reece loved her. She could feel it, even if he could not express it. And she loved him back, as she had always had, ever since she was a child. She had always loved him, and she could never let go.

Just as she could not let go now. Stara knew that he was a world away now, that she should let him go, assume he was dead. After all, how could he have possibly survived out there? And if he had, how would he ever find her?

She hated Thorgrin for this—why couldn't he have gone alone to find his son? Why had he had to drag Reece into this, Legion brother or not?

Yet no matter how hard she tried to shake Reece from her mind, to move on, every day since, Stara thought of nothing but Reece, when he would come back, when she would see him again. It was tearing her up inside. And now, finally, here, so far from anything, so well-hidden, reality was starting to sink in. She would never see Reece again. He would never come for her. He would never find her.

And that was a reality she could not accept.

Stara stormed inside as she walked, determined to find an answer. There had to be a way. There had to be some way to find him.

Otherwise, life meant nothing to her. She refused to spend the rest of her days hiding in this peaceful place of the Ridge, while Reece was out there, in danger. This place, even with all its beauty, held no peace for her as long as Reece was not in it.

"Those are peonies, my lady," came a voice.

Stara turned, surprised, caught off guard by the voice, and was startled to see a member of the royal family standing before her, smiling. From his proud jawline and glistening blue eyes, she could see the resemblance to the King's family, though he was not an immediate member that she could recognize; he looked to be no older than sixteen, dressed in the royal garb of the court.

The man reached forward, smiled, took her hand, and kissed it, a twinkle in his eye.

"They are the finest flowers in court, my lady," he added. "You have fine taste."

He stared at her, and she recognized that look in his eyes. She had seen it on too many suitors over the years: the look of a man captivated by her beauty. It bored her. And in fact, she resented it, given her preoccupation with Reece.

"My name is Fithe," he said. "I am a member of the royal family."

"Are you?" she asked. "You wear the colors, yet at the feast I did not see you seated at the King's table. Nor are you one of the King's sons."

He smiled.

"You are quite perceptive," he replied. "You are correct. I am his nephew—one of them, at least—hardly afforded the privileges of the sons, but a cousin to them nonetheless. But at least I am allowed in the Royal Gardens, which has led me to you."

He smiled wide and Stara turned away, so bored by men's advances upon her. He was nice enough, but speaking to him was the last thing she wanted.

She turned her back and went back to examining the rows of flowers, strolling along them, wanting peace and quiet, wanting to think of Reece and nothing else.

He began to walk alongside her, and she sighed loudly, making it clear she was annoyed.

"I would prefer the pleasure of my own company," she said curtly.

"I meant not to offend, my lady," he said, still walking beside her. "It is just…I could not help but notice you since you arrived here the Ridge. I have been waiting for a moment to talk to you. Your beauty surpasses even what others say."

She looked away, sighing, not wanting to talk to him.

"Please, my lady," he pressed. "I mean you no harm. I would like only to talk to you, to spend some time with you. Allow me to at least show you our royal city."

She faced him, frowning.

"I have seen your city," she replied. "Enough of it, anyway. I care not for it. I had rather wished I had died in the Waste."

He gasped, caught off guard. He looked back at her, surprised; clearly he was not used to women speaking to him this way.

"I wish for nothing here," she replied. "There remains but one thing I wish for in this world, and it is something you could never give me. So you had best leave me be."

He surprised her by staying put and staring back at her, his eyes not filled with scorn or anger but compassion.

"And what is it that you wish for?" he asked. "Simply tell me, and it will be yours."

She looked at him, surprised, her interest piqued.

"I doubt it," she said. "But if you care so much then I will tell you: I want the love of my life returned to me."

She expected him to walk away, and was surprised as he stood there and stared at her, his brow furrowed.

"And where is he?" he asked.

Stara did not expect him to ask her that, or to even care, now that it was clear that she wasn't interested.

"Reece is far from here," she said, "beyond the Great Waste, beyond the sea. He is a castaway, I presume, at sea, on a ship. If he lives at all."

He looked at her for a long time and Stara waited, expecting him to laugh, to walk away, to be rid of her—which was partially what she wanted.

So she was shocked when he finally responded, in all earnestness:

"You love him very much, don't you?" he asked her.

Stara was taken aback by his sincerity, and to see his eyes well with tears.

"Yes," she replied, feeling her own eyes tear up, "I do."

Fithe grew silent, looking down; he seemed to consider her request for a long time.

Finally, he looked back up at her and nodded.

"I will help you," he said.

She studied him, speechless.

"You will?" she asked, feeling her heart beat faster.

"I respect your love, your devotion," he said to her. "I would have loved to have loved you, but I see you are committed to another. And if I cannot have you, then I will have the next best thing: a place in your heart for having helped you."

Stara stared back, touched. For the first time, she felt her heart fill with hope.

"We have strict rules here in the Ridge," he continued. "For our self-preservation. One cannot just leave the Ridge. It would leave a trail for the Empire to find, and endanger us all. Leaving this place is no small feat; if caught, you will be imprisoned, and I along with you."

She nodded back.

"I know," she replied. "I do not expect you to help me."

"I will, though," he said.

She examined him, saw his sincerity, and tried to understand.

"You would risk imprisonment for me?" she asked. "You don't even know me."

He smiled.

"True, I do not," he said. "But I feel in my heart as if I do."

"And yet it sounds as if there is no way," she said. "I want to find him, and to do so, I must leave the Ridge."

"You would have to broach the mountains, to cross the Waste, to find a boat, to set sail at sea alone…" he said. "It is no easy feat."

"I care not," she said. "None of those things frightens me."

He nodded.

"Very well, then," he said. "If your heart is filled enough, then there is always a way."

He held out a single hand, and looked at her with all his intensity.

"Come with me."

Stara placed her hand in his, and as he led her back out, through the gardens, she felt for the first time a new sense of purpose in life, felt that finally, whatever the risk, she would be reunited with Reece again.

CHAPTER TWENTY FOUR

Godfrey stood there, surrounded by a room of hostile Empire soldiers, expecting to be killed—when suddenly, a great horn sounded, shaking the room. It came from somewhere in the distance, persistent, sounding again and again, a dark, foreboding sound, something the likes of which Godfrey had never heard—and the soldiers all turned as one and ran from the room.

Godfrey stood there, sweating, perplexed, staring out at an empty room—only Akorth, Fulton, Merek, and Ario beside him, along with the bartender behind the bar.

Godfrey turned to the others but they all stared back, equally baffled.

"The horns of war," the bartender explained, stopping what he was doing, his voice grave.

"What does it mean?" Merek said.

The bartender shook his head.

"An enemy is at the gates. Volusia is under siege."

Godfrey raced from the tavern with the others, all of them bursting out onto the streets of Volusia. Godfrey was dimly aware of how lucky he had been the war horns had sounded when they had, sparing him from a sure pummeling or even death back in the tavern. Yet as he ran through the panic-filled streets, he was not so sure of his good fortune. He saw thousands of Volusian soldiers mobilizing, racing to the city gates, locking and bolting them and preparing for war.

They all ran toward the city gates, all eager to see what was happening, and as he got closer and burst out of an alleyway, Godfrey finally got a peek through the city gates—and as he did, his heart stopped at the sight: there, lining the horizon, were tens of thousands of Empire soldiers, dressed in their all-black armor, hoisting the banners of the Empire—and marching right for Volusia.

Godfrey had never seen an army that size, and the way they marched, so disciplined, he could see it was a professional army. They bore professional siege equipment, too, rolled on massive wooden platforms, along with a host of catapults—and Godfrey realized that they intended not only to conquer this city—but to obliterate it.

Godfrey was baffled. He did not understand why the Empire army would march on an Empire city, what business they possibly had here. Had the Empire erupted into a civil war?

Godfrey scanned the city and amidst the chaos saw the slaves of Volusia all being auctioned off in the city squares, saw thousands more slaves in the streets, being led to the auction block—and he remembered who the real enemy was. The Volusians. The Empire wanted to destroy this city—and so did he. He wanted all these slaves set free, and perhaps, he realized, this was his opportunity.

The conquerors at the gates, he knew, might be worse than the conquerors here; but if these Volusians prevailed, the slaves would never be free. Besides, Godfrey desperately wanted revenge for Darius and his people. This was as good of a chance as he was going to get.

Spears and arrows began to fly through the iron bars of the city gate, and Volusian soldiers began to cry out and fall as they crisscrossed the courtyard to take up positions all along the city walls. Volusian soldiers, meticulously disciplined, marched single file along the ramparts, obeying the shouts of their commanders, taking up positions. They prepared cauldrons of burning oil and they knelt and fired bows and hurled spears, killing scores of soldiers on the far side of the gates. It was a massive army invading, but it was a massive city they attacked, well-fortified, and Godfrey knew this would be an epic battle. It could go on for months.

Unless he had something to say about it.

Godfrey and the others knelt in the shadows, along a city wall, all of them looking out, watching the war unfold before them. Godfrey exchanged a look with the others.

"Are you thinking what I'm thinking?" Merek asked with a mischievous smile.

Godfrey smiled back.

"And what might that be?" Akorth chimed in, worried.

"Let the Empire in," Godfrey explained. "Let them have the run of the city."

"That is madness!" Fulton said. "They might kill us!"

Godfrey shrugged.

"The Volusians will definitely kill us," he replied. "The Empire might not. And if they do, at least this way they will kill the Volusians first, exact our revenge for us, and we can free these slaves."

Akorth and Fulton, panicked, frowned and shook their heads.

"And how do you propose we do that?" Ario asked, calm and collected, as always.

Godfrey watched the Volusian soldiers turning the huge crank to the gates again and again, beginning to close the massive golden doors behind the city gates—and he had an idea. He leaned over and stroked Dray's head.

"Dray," he commanded. "Go. Avenge Darius. Attack those men!"

Dray needed no prodding: he barked and bolted across the courtyard, doing exactly as Godfrey bid, raising up a cloud of dust as he left a trail.

Dray reached the first soldier and sank his teeth into his ankles—and the soldier cried out, dropping the crank.

"NOW!" Godfrey said.

Godfrey rose to his feet and charged, and the others followed on his heels, Akorth and Fulton, huffing, trailing the group.

They reached the crank and all grabbed hold of it—but could not budge it.

"Turn it the other way!" Godfrey said.

They all turned it the other way, and as Godfrey pulled with all his might, slowly, the city gates began to re-open.

Soon, Volusians caught on. Godfrey ducked as a spear flew by his head, and as he looked up, he saw a squad of Volusians locking eyes on them and tearing off down the ramparts right for them.

"LOOK OUT!" Ario yelled.

Ario picked up a spear, took aim, and hurled it—pushing Godfrey's head down just in time to miss a throwing ax. Godfrey turned to see the spear impale a Volusian soldier a few feet away, attacking them from behind.

Merek drew his sword and killed another Volusian as he attacked them from the other direction.

They all focused again on the crank, and Godfrey kept turning, his hands burning, determined not to let go. He knew, though, that their time was limited, the pack of Volusians bearing down and getting closer with every moment. The door opened wider and wider, moving at a snail's pace.

Godfrey looked up and saw the Volusians were but feet away, about to kill them—but still he would not abandon the crank. He heaved one last time, with all the others, and finally, the gates opened just wide enough.

There came a great shout as there appeared, rushing through the open gates, hundreds of Empire soldiers, streaming in. The Volusian soldiers, overrun, had no recourse but to turn and flee as the momentum pushed them back into their own city. Before their eyes, Volusians were slaughtered, hacked down by the pursuing Empire army, and finally Godfrey felt vindicated. He recalled Darius and his men, butchered in these very same streets by the Volusians—and he knew there was justice in the world.

Godfrey knew that, in the chaos, this was their chance to escape this city.

"Let us go!" Akorth urged, pointing to the rear alleys which could lead to freedom.

Godfrey wanted to leave this place, he truly did.

But he knew he could not. Silis, the Finian woman, would be vulnerable in this invasion. If they did not help her, she would be dead. She had saved him—and he owed her.

"No!" Godfrey called out. "Not yet. We have an obligation to fulfill first. Follow me!"

He turned and ran across the courtyard, Dray barking at his heels, hoping the others would follow—but determined to proceed, even if they did not. For the first time in his life, it was not personal gain that was driving him—but valor. Duty.

He heard footsteps and turned to see the others right behind him, all of them determined, whatever the cost, to do the right thing.

CHAPTER TWENTY FIVE

Kendrick raced with the others across the Great Waste, fighting the sunset, all of them hurrying to make it back in time and knowing what was at stake if they did not. The temperature was beginning to drop dramatically, the light dimming with each passing moment, and Kendrick recalled what the nights were like in the Great Waste. Each night spent here, you took your life in your hands.

Though they had survived in the past, Kendrick knew it would be different this time; here, closer to the Ridge, the nights were more treacherous. Each time he had laid down to sleep he had woken to find a few of his men dead, either eaten by insects, or by strange creatures of the night that disappeared, leaving nothing but bite marks.

Kendrick glanced back over his shoulder and saw the sweepers attached to the rear of the horses, broad and wide, covering their tracks as they went, removing all sign that they'd ever been here. They were ingenious devices, and Kendrick felt at least a sense of satisfaction that they were accomplishing their mission. By the time they reached the Ridge, there would be no sign they'd ever been here, and any danger he and his people had caused by arriving here would be erased.

Kendrick looked over as he rode and saw the bloody corpse of the Ridge soldier, draped along the back of a horse, and his heart went out for him. Because of him and his people, this brave soldier had traveled out here, and now lay dead. Kendrick could not but help feel responsible—even if he personally had saved many of their lives.

Kendrick spotted Naten riding before his men, a permanent sneer on his face, still not looking Kendrick's way. Even though Kendrick had saved his life, he'd received nothing but bitterness in return. Some people, Kendrick knew, would always be the way they were. And yet, Kendrick noticed a shift in the attitude of the other members of the Ridge toward him. Ever since the fighting back at the twisted tree, since he had helped save them as if they were his own, they had looked upon him with a new respect. He knew that slowly, they were coming to accept him, even though he was an outsider.

They charged and charged, the sound of horses thumping in his ears, and Kendrick scoured the horizon for any sign of the Sand Wall, knowing it was the first landmark he needed to see. Yet he was frustrated to find it was always out of view.

A shout suddenly rang out above the din of the horses, and Kendrick was surprised as he looked over and saw one of the soldiers of the Ridge suddenly fall from his horse as it collapsed beneath him. They both rolled on the ground, as the others all ground to a halt, and Kendrick was baffled. At first he assumed the horse had tripped—but he did not see how, given the flat landscape.

But then he was shocked to see another horse collapse—and then another—sending its riders down to the ground, the first rider shrieking as he was crushed beneath the horse.

Soon there was an avalanche of horses collapsing, rolling, sending up huge clouds of dust.

Kendrick veered out of the way of all the fallen horses, just in time, and just as he thought he was safe, suddenly his own horse inexplicably collapsed out from under him, and Kendrick felt himself go flying, face first, onto the hard desert floor. Riding at the speed he was it was a hard landing, making him winded and feel as if he had broken every bone in his body.

Kendrick rolled and rolled, coughing up dust, quickly evading his horse is it rolled past him, and wondering what on earth could have happened.

As he came to a stop, breathing hard, grabbing his ribs, he turned and examined the desert floor, wondering if they'd ridden into a series of cracks.

But there were no cracks anywhere. The ground was as smooth as could be.

The mystery only deepened as Kendrick looked around and heard the horses neighing, as if in pain, and then heard an awful buzzing sound. He looked closely and was horrified to see the horses' legs were all covered in swarming bugs—eating them alive.

The horses neighed and writhed as their flesh was being eaten, and Kendrick reacted, jumping to his feet, drawing his sword, and swinging at the horses' legs, trying to get them off.

Kendrick quickly realized that swinging his sword was ineffective, as he could not risk hurting the horses. He reached for a shield instead—but by the time he turned around, it was already too late: the bugs were so vicious, so well-coordinated, they had already eaten most of the horses' legs, swarming so fast that before Kendrick's eyes their legs began to disappear. Within seconds, they had eaten their legs down to the bone.

Kendrick could not believe it. As he watched, before his eyes, the horses, now entirely swarmed by bugs, became nothing but bones, fossils, as if they had been on the desert floor for thousands of years.

Just as quickly, the swarm of bugs lifted up from the bones and flew away in a giant blur, blackening the sky before they disappeared in a cloud.

Kendrick stood and as he dusted himself off, exchanged a look with the others—who all stared back, equally shocked. He looked down at the carcasses of the horses and he realized with a pit in his stomach that they now had no means of transportation back to the Ridge. He looked out at the horizon, at the setting sun, and the Ridge now felt very far away. He could not believe he was finding himself back in the same position, being back out in the Great Waste, on foot. He felt the temperature dropping, and he knew they were all in a very bad position.

"This is *your* fault!"

Kendrick turned to see Naten, enraged, charging for him.

Kendrick was too shocked to react, and before he knew it, Naten was on top of him, tackling him and driving him down to the ground.

The others circled around and began cheering them on, as Kendrick found himself in a wrestling match. Naten, on top of him, pinned him down then reached out and tried to choke him. Kendrick felt strong hands on his throat and realized this was serious. He was tired of pacifying this man.

Kendrick, enraged, reached up and pushed a pressure point on the man's forearms; immediately Naten released his grip, and Kendrick then swatted them off to the side, at the same time raising his head and head-butting his nose.

Naten, stunned, clutched his nose and rolled to the side.

Kendrick rolled away and gained his feet, and Naten, bouncing back, gained his, too. The two faced each other in the midst of the circle of soldiers.

Naten, enraged, drew his sword, the sound cutting through the desert air—but before he could take a step, Brandt and Atme appeared, each holding the tip of their swords at his throat.

"Go no further," Brandt warned.

"That is our commander whom you threaten," Atme added.

The sound of more drawn swords filled the air, and Kendrick looked over to see two soldiers of the Ridge, friends of Naten's, drawing their swords and pointing them at Brandt and Atme.

"Lower your swords!" Koldo yelled to his own men, stepping forward angrily.

"And you lower yours," Kendrick said to Brandt and Atme. "I thank you, but we are not here to fight each other."

The two Ridge soldiers lowered theirs, and Brandt and Atme followed, and soon it was only Naten who held a sword.

"I said lower it," Koldo growled, sneering down at him, getting in his face.

Reluctantly, Naten lowered his.

Kendrick stood there and faced Naten, who glared back, bleeding from his lip.

"Friend," Kendrick called out, determined to bring peace. "You cannot blame me for your friend's death, or for these horses' death. I am not the enemy. If you recall, it was *I* who saved your life but hours ago."

Naten sneered.

"If it weren't for you or your men showing up here, my men would be alive," Naten said. "Our horses would still live, and we would not be in this mess. Now we are all going to die out here."

"Blame is an easy thing," Kendrick replied. "It is the weapon of the least accomplished man. I don't know about you," Kendrick said, turning to the others, "but I don't plan on dying. We will find a way back to the Ridge. I do not wish to fight you, or your people. I volunteered on this mission to help."

Kendrick decided he would be the bigger man. As all the soldiers watched, he held out a hand for peace, stepping forward to shake Naten's hand.

Naten stood there, the silence so thick one could cut it with a knife. He stared back, as if deliberating.

"Shake his hand," Koldo commanded.

But Naten sneered, spit down at Kendrick's foot, turned, and stormed away.

Kendrick expected no less.

Koldo came up beside him and placed a hand on his shoulder.

"You are a fine man," he said. "The bigger man. Thank you for your restraint."

Kendrick nodded back, appreciating the sentiment.

"As it is, we would be lucky to survive this," Ludvig said, coming up beside him. "If we turn on each other, we stand no chance at all."

Kendrick turned with the others and looked out at the setting sun, and he knew their situation was bleak.

Kendrick turned to his men.

"Gather what you can from the shells of your horses," he said. "Tonight, we camp here."

Koldo commanded his men, too, and soon all the men were scouring the saddles, lying on the ground, rummaging through their horses' bones; others gathered dried sticks and weeds from the desert floor, and soon a pile for a bonfire was assembled.

The sky grew darker and Kendrick looked up at the last glimmer of light, and despite himself, he felt a chill: he could not help feeling, like the others, that they would never make it back.

*

Kendrick sat around the raging bonfire, the only light in the sea of desert darkness, beside him Brandt, Atme and his men, while Koldo, Ludvig, and the others sat around the circle to his other side. They were all on edge. There was no sound in the desert save for the crackling of the wood, and the frigid air had crept in, the flames of the fire the only thing keeping it at bay. Kendrick, drained from the day's events, looked out at the faces of the other men, all around the fire, and could see the weariness in them, too. They had all found themselves in a situation that none of them had expected to be in.

Kendrick stared into the flames, reflecting on how life had brought him to this point, and felt his eyes growing heavy when a fierce sound punctured the silence. Kendrick felt the hairs rise on the back of his neck as he turned with the others and peered out into the blackness. It came again: the distant screech of a creature, somewhere out there.

Kaden, the King's youngest son and the youngest of the group, sitting close to Kendrick, flinched at the sound and grabbed the hilt of his sword.

Naten laughed cruelly and lashed out at him: "What are you scared of, boy?" Naten mocked. "You afraid that thing's gonna come eat you?"

A few of the other soldiers chuckled, while Kaden reddened.

"I'm not scared of anything," Kaden said indignantly.

Naten laughed again.

"You look scared to me."

Kaden sat up straighter and scowled.

"Whatever it is, it can come here, and I shall face it fearlessly," he insisted.

Naten scoffed.

"I'm sure you will," he said.

Kendrick could see Kaden's embarrassment and he felt badly for him—and angry at Naten for being the bully who he was.

The screech came again, but more distant this time, whatever it was, receding back into the night; they all gradually settled back into the silence.

"I don't know how you all managed to survive out there," came a voice.

Kendrick turned to see Kaden looking back at him; he had an affable and friendly face, earnest, quick to smile, and filled with the confidence of a fourteen-year-old boy who had more courage than battle skills. Kendrick could spot in him the warrior that he would become, could see his eagerness to prove himself.

Kendrick grinned back.

"We were trained for adversity," Kendrick replied. He could see other soldiers looking his way, curious, and as he spoke, he addressed them all. "Back in the Ring, we were sent on patrols from the time we could walk. When joining the Legion, and then the Silver, we were sent to the most awful places—the base of the Canyon, the heart of the Wilds—for moons at a time, forced to be thrown into the most hostile savage lands. It was our initiation ritual. Not all came back. But it taught us to live without fear of safety or security. Our security became our two hands, and the weapons we bore."

Koldo nodded, clearly appreciating the story.

"We have a similar ritual," Koldo said. "We send our young initiates on patrols at the peak of the Ridge. *Wolves*, we call them."

"But the Ridge is secluded," Kendrick said. "What are they patrolling for?"

"On occasion," Koldo replied, "desert creatures cross the sand wall, and try to broach the walls of the Ridge. We must maintain lookouts, all day and night, on all peaks of the Ridge. When they cross, we send out patrols to battle these monsters, before they get too close. It keeps the Ridge safe, and it keeps us battle hardened. They are vicious foes, and they attack in packs, worse foes, even, than the Empire."

"You would not know," Naten interjected. "None of you precious Silver have ever been tested against our foes."

"They have had to contend with foes, I am sure, far deadlier than they," Ludvig interjected, standing up for Kendrick.

Kendrick nodded back, appreciating that, and Naten merely shrugged.

"*I* will be a Wolf soon," Kaden said proudly. "My coming-of-age ritual will be next. I will patrol the Ridge, with but a few friends. We will fight and kill any creatures we find."

Kendrick smiled, admiring his courage.

"So this then is your first time out in the Waste?" Kendrick asked.

Kaden nodded back solemnly.

"I volunteered," he said. "My father refused at first, but my brother allowed it and convinced him to let me."

Koldo turned to Kendrick.

"We treat our young here," Koldo said, "with the greatest respect. In our kingdom, the greatest honor is reserved for the youngest. It is the youngest son, not the eldest, who holds all of our pride and joy. For however the youngest fights is a reflection upon not only his father but his older brothers. We must all be an example of honor and courage, and that must be found in the youngest. The coming-of-age ritual is something we hold with the highest regard."

"Our boy warriors," Ludvig added, "reflect what is best in us. The time of life when one evolves from a boy to a man is a very sacred time. It is, in fact, the most important time for our people."

A comfortable silence fell over the group of warriors, and as the fire crackled, Kendrick became lost in thought, his eyes heavy, until Kaden turned to him.

"What is it that you live for now?" Kaden asked.

Kendrick turned to him and could see this earnest boy was struggling to understand.

"Your beloved homeland is gone," Kaden continued. "Your men are mostly dead. I cannot imagine going on. What is it that keeps you going? Was it that you wish for?"

Kendrick thought long and hard about that. It made him miss the Ring, and his fellow Silver, more than ever before.

"I live to, one day, return to my homeland," Kendrick finally replied. "To see the Ring restored once again. To see the Silver's ranks replenished. For our men to become the great army and the great knights that we once were."

The men nodded back, respecting his response.

"And yet," Kendrick added, "I've also learned that being a knight means being a knight wherever you are. In whatever place, and whatever circumstance. I have learned that I do not need to be in the Ring, in King's Court, in a fine castle and city, or even in my armor. That is not what it means to be a knight. The true knight leaves all those things behind; he is out there fighting for a cause, and that cause is always outside his well-fortified city gate. When you are out there, somewhere, in the heart of the dangers, when you feel as if you are in the loneliest and emptiest place of all, when you look around and there is no one left to your left or to your right, when you are forging new ground—that is when you are taking up the cause of the true knight. That is what you make your home. The true knight has no home—he forges his home. And he is always forging a new one. And that is where my home lies now."

"I'll drink to that," Ludvig said.

He raised his sack, and Kendrick and the others raised theirs, as they all drank around the fire.

"To honor!" Koldo called out.

"To honor!"

Kendrick took a long drink of his wine, staring into the flames, as he dwelled on the final word. *Honor.* That, above all, was what he lived for.

"I understand how you feel, my friend," Koldo said, in his deep voice, beside him. "I myself was once an outsider to this place."

Kendrick looked back at him, wondering. Given Koldo's black skin, his appearance so different from everyone here, and his being the King's eldest son, Kendrick had always wondered about him. But he had never wanted to pry.

"As you can tell," Koldo continued, "I was not born of the King, or the Queen. They found me, in the Waste, on a King's patrol, and they took me in as their own. Even more so, being their eldest, they named me their firstborn—and heir to the kingdom. They have made me the eldest in every sense of the word, even when they didn't need to. That is what these people of the Ridge are made of."

Kendrick was intrigued by his story.

"They found you?" he asked. "How?"

"The King and his men once raided a slave village, deep in the Waste, to kill Empire soldiers who had gotten too close, and to liberate the slaves. When they got there, the Empire had already left, and the village was smoldering. Everyone was dead—except for me. They could have left me there, for dead. But that is our King, my father, my true father: he has a big heart, and he does what is right."

Koldo sighed.

"I do not forget. I never forget, when it comes to loyalty. I would die for our King in the blink of an eye. I would lead his men anywhere, anywhere in the world he wants them to go."

"Koldo is my brother," Ludvig said. "My true brother. He might be born of different parents, have a different skin color than I, but that means nothing. That is not what it means to be a brother. His honor and courage and loyalty are what make him my brother. I consider him my blood, as I do my other brothers, and I would die for him in the blink of an eye."

"As would I," said Kaden. "Koldo is as much my brother as Ludvig."

Kendrick could see the intense loyalty Koldo inspired, and he admired it greatly. It made him think back to King MacGil, who had taken him in as his son. MacGil wanted to name Kendrick his firstborn, his heir—but that had been his one failing: he had never been strong enough to overcome the customs of his people, to allow a bastard to be King. The King of the Ridge, though, Kendrick could see, was different: he had defied tradition to do what was right. Kendrick longed for a father like that.

"I suppose we have something in common," Kendrick said. "We were both raised by parents not our own. Yet somehow we have both risen to become leaders of our troops."

Koldo smiled back, the first time Kendrick had seen him smile.

"What is it that they say?" Koldo asked. "That it is always the outsiders, the ones least accepted, the ones that people expect nothing of, that rise to the top."

Kendrick understood—more than he could say.

CHAPTER TWENTY SIX

Volusia stepped out from the shadows into the bright sunlight and onto her private terrace in the coliseum—and as she did, the crowd went wild. She stood there and raised her arms and turned every which way as she took in the cheers and adulation from thousands of adoring fans, all citizens of her capital city. The stadium roared and shook at her very presence, and she knew that they loved her. She, the conquering hero. They loved her strength; they loved her power. She, whom no one had ever expected anything of. Finally, they had come to learn what she had known all along: that she was a goddess. That she was invincible.

Already the statues of her were ubiquitous in the city, the morning prayer rituals to her image had been set, and the people bowed down to her everywhere she went. Yet it was still not enough for her. She wanted more.

If her people didn't genuinely love her, Volusia knew, when they saw her face they wouldn't cheer as they dead, wouldn't shower her with affection. It was not just from fear, but from awe. She could feel it. She had conquered the city that could not be conquered, had taken the throne which could not be taken. She had proved them all wrong, and they loved her for it. They knew with her, everything was possible.

Volusia held out her arms, and as she did, trumpets sounded. Slowly, the crowd quieted. They all looked to her, so silent and respectful that one could hear a pin drop.

"Citizens of the Empire!" she called out, her voice booming, echoing off the walls. "People of my capital city! You are subjects no more. You are now free! Free to serve not many, not commanders, not soldiers—but only the Goddess Volusia."

The crowd cheered, stomping up and down the rows, and it went on so long, Volusia was certain it would never end.

Finally, she raised her arms again and they quieted.

"As my gift to you," she boomed, "as my gift for liberating your great city, I present to you what no leader before me has ever given you: one hundred days of games! Let the bloodsport begin!"

Trumpets sounded as the crowd shrieked with delight, the entire stadium shaking in a frenzy. Volusia receded from the light, back into the shadows, and sat on the edge of her terrace on her golden throne, flanked by her advisors, and watched down over all of it.

Far below, the great iron doors to the arena opened, with a groan so loud it drowned out even the chanting of the crowd, and as it did, the first day's gladiators, shackled to one another, were brought out. The crowd went wild as dozens of gladiators came stumbling into the center of the arena, looking in every direction, panicked.

A horn sounded, another door opened, and out rode dozens of Empire soldiers, riding zertas, their black armor glistening beneath the suns, and wielding sharpened spears. They charged right for the group, and the crowd cheered them on as the first of the spears were hurled through the air.

Soon the air was filled with dozen of spears, all aimed down at the panicked gladiators, raining down on them from all directions.

The gladiators tried to turn and run, bumping into each other—but there was nowhere for them to go.

Soon, they were all impaled. Some tried to duck, while others dove for the ground—but these were just impaled through their backs. Others raised their petty shields—but the spears, so sharp, just went right through. Death was everywhere—and it found them.

As the crowd cheered, the riders circled around, bent down low, and grabbed the chains binding the gladiators together—then dragged them along the ground, parading their trophies around the arena. The crowd stood and roared as they passed.

A horn sounded, another gate opened, and yet another group of gladiators were ushered into the arena.

Volusia took in all the cruelty on display, and it brightened her mood. Indeed, this particularly vicious arena, here in the capital, was one of the reasons she had wanted to take the capital to begin with. Watching people die in unusual ways was one of her favorite hobbies.

"Goddess," came a voice.

Volusia, annoyed at being interrupted, turned to see Rory, the new commander of her forces, looking back at her with concern. She had given him the title after killing the previous three commanders on a whim. She felt it was always good to keep her men on their toes.

"Goddess, forgive me for interrupting you," he said, worry in his voice.

"I do *not* forgive you," she said coldly. "I do not forgive interruptions."

He gulped.

"Goddess, I beg your forgiveness. But it is urgent."

She stared back at him.

"Nothing is urgent in my world. I am a Goddess."

He looked uncertain whether to continue.

"I bear news, Goddess," he said. "Romulus's million men, fresh from the Ring, are nearing our shores in a vast fleet. They approach the Western Bay, even now, as we speak—and we have no planned defenses for them. By tomorrow, our capital will be overrun."

She stared back evenly.

"And what is urgent?" she asked.

He blinked, speechless.

"Goddess," he continued, unsure, "there are only two ways for us to flee the capital—to the west or the east. With the Knights of the Seven and their millions of men advancing from the east, we have only the western escape—and now that exit is trapped by Romulus's million men. We are surrounded, with nowhere to flee."

Volusia stared back evenly, hearing the distant roar of the crowd, and annoyed that she was being distracted, that she was turned away from seeing whoever was just killed.

"And whoever said anything about fleeing?" she asked.

He looked back, dumbfounded.

"I never retreat, Commander," she said.

"But something must be done!" he said urgently.

She smiled wide. Finally, she rose and walked from the terrace, wanting to hear no more of this.

"Follow me," she said.

*

Volusia approached the shore of the Western Bay, flanked by her huge entourage of advisors and generals and commanders, walking quickly out in front of them, as she stepped across the beach of small rocks, heading towards the water's edge. The water lapped lightly, and in the distance, against the cloudy afternoon and the streaks of a glowing sunset, she saw the sea of Romulus's ships, freshly back from the Ring, even with their precious Romulus dead, all coming together in common cause, clearly at the behest of the Knights of the Seven. They still thought the Seven were in control; they still did not realize that the Empire was hers now.

Volusia felt honored that all these men would mobilize from halfway around the world, that they would vacate their precious Ring, just for her. And she pitied them. They had no idea that they were up against a Goddess. That she was untouchable.

"Do you see, Goddess?" Rory continued, panic in his rising voice. "We must mobilize our men, quickly! We waste precious time!"

Volusia, ignoring him, marched out ahead of her men, right down to the water's edge. She stood there, lifted her chin, and felt the strong winds in her face, and welcomed them. They cooled off the heat of the desert, of the unbearably hot morning in the capital.

Volusia heard the distant drumbeat of the warships, pounding incessantly in the distance, as if to frighten her, and she watched as the ships all began to enter the bay. As if these fools really believed they could scare her.

Volusia stood there, one woman against an army, and watched as they came in, ever closer, filling the massive bay, blocking her exit west—just as she wanted them to.

"Goddess!" Rory blank repeated. "We must retreat!"

Volusia looked up and saw the torches on all the ships, all the flaming arrows, all spears, all the men waiting only to get in range. She knew that in but a few minutes they would rain down a hell upon her and all her men, a wave of death and destruction.

Yet she had other plans—she was not prepared to die just yet. And certainly not by these men's hands, the remnant of a mediocre commander, Romulus, her predecessor, and a fool.

Volusia turned and nodded to Volk, who stood beside her. He nodded back, and several of his small, green men rushed forward, making squealing noises, anathema even to her. They slowly raised their hands and held them out before them, their fingers spread in a triangle shape as they aimed them at the sea.

Slowly, a green glow spread from their palms; it oozed over the waters like a slime, spreading and spreading, until it crept beneath Romulus's ships. The Volks then turned their palms slowly upward, lifted them higher and higher.

As they did, they summoned forth creatures from the deep, raising them up higher and higher, from the black sea. Slowly, the entire water filled with small, green glowing crabs, making an awful clattering noise as they spread out and clung to the hulls of all the ships.

They crawled up the hulls, covering them like ants, and as they did there came the sound of creaking and splintering wood. They were eating away at the ships, like piranhas, and splinters began to fly everywhere.

Volusia looked on in satisfaction, as one after another all the ships began to list, then teeter—then collapse. They crumbled into the water, their hulls eaten out from under them.

Men shrieked, an awful sound, as thousands upon thousands fell, flailing through the air and into the water. As they did, they were met by thousands of crabs, waiting. The shrieks became even more awful as soon the waters turned red with the blood of Romulus's million men.

Volusia stood there, grinning, taking it all in with satisfaction.

She turned and looked at the face of her shocked commanders.

"Now," she said, "I shall return to my games."

CHAPTER TWENTY SEVEN

Godfrey ran, Merek, Ario, Akorth, and Fulton beside him, out from the shadows of the city courtyard, away from the Empire army pouring through the gates, determined to save Silis. As he reached an alleyway and prepared to duck into it, he turned back and looked. He was both delighted and scared to see the hordes of Empire soldiers rushing through the gates, slaughtering Volusian soldiers left and right. On the one hand, it was all thanks to him and his men, and it was exactly what he wanted; on the other hand, the storm he had unleashed looked like it was going to kill everything in its path—including him.

He still could not understand why Empire was fighting Empire, and as he took a close look at their armor, he realized it was a different sort of Empire armor, all black, their helmets with pointy noses. He looked up high, at the banners they were waving, and he noticed they were bearing a different insignia. He struggled to read it.

"What army is this?" Merek asked, wondering aloud the same thing he was.

"Why does Empire kill Empire?" Ario asked.

Godfrey squinted, trying to make out the letters on the banner, written in the ancient language of the Empire; he had been schooled in it as a boy, but he had cut too many classes, sneaking out for the taverns. Now he wished he had studied harder.

Godfrey tried to decipher it through his drunken haze, his heart still pounding, still covered in sweat from their crazy feat of opening the gate and letting these people in. They were getting closer, but he was dying to know who they were before disappearing.

Finally, he made out the insignia, the words: *The Knights of the Seven.*

It all came rushing back to him, all of his history lessons.

"They represent the four horns and two spikes," Godfrey said. "They are from the far side of the Empire. They would not attack Volusia unless she had done something to betray them." He finally understood. "It's a personal vendetta," he added. "They are going to kill everyone here—including us."

Godfrey watched as more men—an endless stream—flooded into the city, slaughtering the overwhelmed Volusians left and right, throwing axes into their backs as they ran, trampling them with their horses, a great army of death and destruction taking over the city like ants. He watched as the army approached a group of slaves, and he was hopeful to see them liberate them. But he was shocked and outraged to watch the Empire army slaughter the defenseless slaves, too, all shackled to each other in their path.

Maybe, Godfrey wondered, he should never have let them in. Perhaps they were even worse than the Volusians.

"They haven't come to liberate us," Akorth said. "But to murder everything in sight!"

Godfrey, thinking the same thing, watched them topple an immense statue of Volusia: the fifty-foot statue, made of marble, slowly fell, landing on top of dozens of Volusian soldiers, crushing them and shattering with a huge explosion, the pieces scattering in every direction. Another division of soldiers rushed forward and began setting fire to everything in sight.

"There!" Akorth yelled.

Godfrey turned and saw him pointing to the harbor on the far side of the courtyard; there was a row of ships, sitting there empty.

"We can make it to the harbor!" he added. "We can still slip out in the confusion, before anyone knows we are here. This is our chance!"

They all looked to Godfrey, and Godfrey knew they were right. They were at a crossroads: to their left, the alleyways, and a chance to free Silis. To their right, finally, freedom.

Not long ago Godfrey would have jumped at the chance for escape, would have run in his drunken haze, jumped on the boat, shoved off, and would have sailed anywhere the tides would take him.

But now, Godfrey was changing; something was stirring within him. Something he hated within himself, but he could not control. Some damn thing which felt a lot like chivalry. Like honor.

"Silis," Godfrey said. "She saved us when she didn't need to. She did right by us," he said, turning to the others, realizing he was speaking from his heart. "We vowed to help her, and we cannot abandon her now. She will die."

"We *have* helped her," Akorth countered. "We have helped destroy her city—she got what she wanted."

Godfrey shook his head.

"She did not want death," he said. "She was not expecting this. They are going to kill her, to kill everyone in sight." Godfrey sighed, hating what he was going to say, but feeling he had no choice. "We cannot turn our backs on her now."

They all gaped at him, disbelieving.

"That is freedom there," Akorth said, pointing, frantic. "Do you not understand?"

"You disappoint me," Fulton said. "You, Godfrey, of all people, infected with this trait called honor?"

Godfrey looked back firmly, resigned.

"I will not leave this city," he said, "not without saving her. If you wish to go, I understand. I won't stop you—and I don't blame you."

The others exchanged a glance, then finally, Akorth shook his head.

"We're too damn stupid to let you die alone," Akorth said.

"If we survive this," Fulton added, "you owe me the best damn drink of my life."

Godfrey smiled wide, as the others clasped him on the shoulder and they all turned and ran, ducking into the alleyways before the army could catch up.

They darted through the alleyways, twisting and turning, taking shortcuts, clinging to the walls and hiding in the shadows, until they finally reached Silis' palace, still safe on the far side of the city. The Empire army had not reached it yet, though Godfrey could hear their shouting not far behind, and he knew they would reach it soon.

Godfrey ran through the wide, arched opening into her palace, running up the steps three at a time, racing past the guards and not stopping as they shouted at him. He ran up floor after floor until finally, gasping for breath, he reached her floor and sprinted down the hall to her chamber, the guards close behind.

He burst open her door, its wood shattering, and found her lying there, relaxing on a chaise lounge. She jumped up, startled, as they all burst in—and at the same time, her guards ran up from behind and grabbed Godfrey.

"What is the meaning of this?" she demanded.

Several more of her guards poured into the room, surrounding Godfrey and his men.

"Volusia is overrun!" Godfrey called out, gasping for breath. "Come with us! Quickly! There is still a chance to escape!"

Silis, eyes widening in shock, turned and rushed to the doors to her balcony and threw them open. As she did, a wave of noise entered the room—the calamitous shouts of men killing and ransacking.

She stepped back from the balcony, horrified, as she looked out, and Godfrey knew she must be witnessing the devastation to her city.

"Let him go," she commanded her men, and Godfrey was relieved to feel the hands off of him.

She turned and examined Godfrey, staring into his eyes, and her face filled with gratitude and surprise.

"You came back for me," she said, realizing. "You risked your lives for me. Why?"

"Because I promised I would," Godfrey replied truthfully.

She laid a soft hand on his wrist.

"I shall never forget this," she said.

"Let's go now!" Merek called out. "We still have a chance to make the ships!"

She shook her head.

"We would never reach them," she said. "We'd never make it out of the harbor."

Godfrey suddenly realized she was right, and realized that by coming here, by acting selflessly, he had actually saved his own life.

She looked at them and spoke earnestly.

"I have the perfect place, built for times like this," she said. "A secret chamber, hidden far beneath this palace. You will join me."

"My lady!" one of her men protested. "There is not room for them all!"

She turned to him coldly.

"They came back for me," she said. "I will make room."

She turned and hurried through the room, and they all followed her as she opened a secret door in the wall and entered a hidden spiral staircase. As Godfrey followed her in with the others, the stone wall closed perfectly behind them, concealing them in the darkness. Silis grabbed a torch from the wall and led them down, flight after flight, deeper and deeper into the blackness. As they went, Godfrey could hear the shouting of the army getting closer, surrounding the palace.

When they finally stopped Godfrey was confused, as the stairs seemed to end in a stone wall. But Silis nodded to her guards, they pulled a lever, and the stone wall slid open, revealing a hidden door, eight feet thick. They pushed it open with all their might, as Godfrey and the others watched, amazed.

Silis turned to them and smiled.

"Loyalty," she said, "has its rewards."

CHAPTER TWENTY EIGHT

Erec stood at the stern of the ship, looking out as the early morning sun broke on the horizon, thrilled to be moving again. Finally back on the river after the long night of festivities, he led his fleet as they continued upriver, toward Volusia. Alistair stood beside him, and Erec reached out and clasped her hand. She looked up at him and smiled, and he felt elated as he thought of their baby girl. It was the greatest honor he could imagine, and it made him feel a new sense of purpose in life.

Erec checked over his shoulder and on the horizon, disappearing, he saw all the villagers, still lined up at the shore, waving their gratitude and goodbye to them. His heart broke as he watched them disappear, recalling how gracious and kind these people had been to him and his men, and how grateful they had been for his liberating them. They waved him on with love even though they knew he was heading to Volusia instead of forking upriver in the other direction to save their neighboring village and help liberate them once and for all. Their unconditional gratitude made him feel even worse.

Erec checked the horizon, and downriver, in the distance, he could begin to see the faint outline of the Empire fleet, thousands of ships, still a good day's ride behind him but closing in fast as they pursued him upriver. Apparently they had broken through the blockade, and now that their fear of traveling by river at night had passed, they had set off at first light of dawn. Erec knew he could not elude them forever: an epic battle loomed on the horizon.

Erec checked his sails, pleased to see them at full ballast, his ship moving quickly as they took the tides upriver. He looked ahead, and as he did, he saw looming quickly, a huge fork in the river. To the right, he knew, the river wound its way to Volusia; to the left, as the villagers had told him, it twisted its way to their sister village, to the Empire fort, to the place they had begged him to go. Erec knew if he forked right and skipped the fort, the villagers back there would surely be dead; and yet if he forked left, it would risk his men's lives, give the

Empire a chance to catch up, and delay his entering Volusia, if at all. He would be imperiling his men for a battle not their own, and on a river filled with monsters. Indeed, even from here, as Erec looked left, he saw the waters in that direction swirling with snakes, even in the daylight.

"What will you decide, my brother?" came a voice.

Erec turned to see Strom standing beside him, hands on hips, looking out at the fork, a concerned expression on his face.

"I know what you are thinking, my brother," Strom continued. "Even though we were separated from childhood, I still know you better than you know yourself. You're thinking you want to go save these villagers. Whatever the cost. Whatever the odds. I know you are, because that is *who you are*."

Erec looked back at him, realizing he was right.

"And you, my brother?" he asked. "Could you do any differently?"

After a long, somber silence, Strom shook his head.

"You and I," he replied, "are the same. Driven by honor. Whatever the cost. It is not only what we do—it is *how we live*."

Erec studied the waters, the fork looming, and knew he was right.

"Though I am the better fighter, of course," Strom added with a smile.

"It would not be a wise decision, my lord."

Erec turned to see one of his trusted commanders, coming up on his other side. He knew he was right.

"Wisdom is important," Erec replied. "But sometimes it must defer to honor. Life is sacred—but honor is more sacred than life."

"Many men will die," the commander added.

Erec nodded.

"All of us will die," Erec replied. "At one time or another. What you still fail to understand is that I do not fear a mission into danger when honor is at stake. Rather I embrace it, with joy, from the bottom of my heart. The challenge, the insurmountable odds of that river, that is what we live for."

Erec looked in front of him, studying the river in the morning silence, the only sound that of the water lapping against the hull, the tides becoming rougher as they neared the fork. Erec glanced back and saw the Empire fleet, much closer already. And he knew what he had to do.

"Full sail ahead!" he yelled, stepping forward, turning the wheel, and directing the ship left, toward the village, away from Volusia.

Erec looked over and saw Alistair's approving face by his side, saw Strom smiling back, his hand already on the hilt of his sword, and he looked back out at the looming fork. As their boat turned away, toward waters unknown, he knew, he just knew, that this was where he was meant to be.

CHAPTER TWENTY NINE

The small group of Empire soldiers charged through the Great Waste, galloping at full speed on their zertas, faster than any horse, and stirring up a massive cloud of dust in their wake. At their head rode their commander, the cruel, merciless Empire veteran who had taken great pleasure in torturing Boku before his last breath—and discovering exactly where Gwendolyn and her crew had departed into the Great Waste.

Now the commander led the small group of Empire trackers deeper and deeper into the Waste, following Gwendolyn's people's trail as it led away from the Empire village, tracking it as they had been for days, determined to discover where she went. The order had trickled down from Volusia herself, and the commander knew that if he did not succeed, it would mean his death. He would have to find her, no matter what, dead or alive. If he could find bring her back to Volusia as a trophy, it would mean his promotion, his rise to commander of one of her armies. For that, he would give anything.

The commander raised his whip and lashed his zerta again across the face, making it scream and not caring. He had driven his men mercilessly, too, not allowing them to sleep, or even stop, for an entire day. They tore through the desert, following the trail that the commander was determined not to allow to go cold. After all, it might not just be Gwen at the end of it; it could even be the famed Ridge, the one that had eluded Empire commanders for centuries. If Gwendolyn's trail lead to that—if it even existed—then he would come back as the greatest hero in modern times. Volusia might then even make him her Supreme Commander.

The commander watched the hard-baked soil as they went, using his keen eyes to look for any variations, any movements. He had already noticed where, miles back, many of Gwendolyn's men had dropped dead. A good tracker knew that a trail was not static, but a living thing, always subject to change—and always telling a story, if one knew how to look.

The commander slowed his zerta as he noticed another change in the trail. It narrowed dramatically up ahead, indicating fewer people, and immersed in the sand, he also saw the remnants of corpses. Up ahead, he saw some bones scattered about, and he brought his zerta to a stop.

His men all came to an abrupt stop beside him.

The commander dismounted, walked over to the bones, long-dried, and knelt beside them. He ran his hand along them, and as he did, he drew on his expertise to look for the signs. The Empire—Volusia herself—had chosen him for this very purpose. In addition to being an expert torturer, he was known as the Empire army's greatest tracker, able to find anyone, anywhere—without fail.

As he fell silent, studying them, his men came up and knelt beside him.

"They are dried," his men said. "These people died moons ago."

The commander studied them, though, and shook his head.

Finally, he replied: "No, not weeks ago. You are deceived. The bones are clean, but not due to time. They have been picked clean by insects. They are actually quite fresh."

The commander picked one up, to demonstrate, and tried to break it in his hand—it did not break.

"It is not as brittle as it seems," he replied.

"But what killed them?" one of his men asked.

He studied the sand around the bones, running his hand through it.

"There was a scuffle here," he finally said. "A fight between men."

His men surveyed the desert floor.

"It looks like they were all killed," one observed.

But the commander was unconvinced: he looked out into the desert, studied the floor, and saw a glimpse of the trail up ahead, however faint it was.

He shook his head and stood to his full height.

"No," he replied decisively. "Some of them survived. The group has splintered. They are weak now. They are hurt—and they are mine."

He jumped onto his zerta, lashed it across the face, and broke off at a gallop, following the trail, eyes locked on it, determined to hunt them down, wherever they were, and kill whoever had survived this group.

*

The commander charged into the afternoon sky, the two suns hanging low as great balls on the horizon, heading ever deeper into the Great Waste. His zerta gasped and his soldiers heaved behind him, all of them on the verge of collapse. The commander did not care. They could all drop dead out here in the desert for all he cared. He wanted only one thing, and he would not stop until he had it: to find Gwendolyn.

The commander fantasized as he rode; he imagined himself finding Gwendolyn alive, torturing her for days on end, then tying her to his zerta and riding back the entire way that way. It would be fun to see how long it would take until it killed her. No, he realized—he could not do that. He would lose his prize. Maybe he would just torture her a little bit.

Or maybe, just maybe, her trail would lead him to the fabled Ridge, the holy grail of the Empire quests. If he found it, he would sneak back and report it to the Empire, and lead an army out here personally to return and destroy it. He smiled wide—he would be famous for generations.

They charged and charged, every bone in his body aching, his throat so dry he could barely breathe, and not caring. The suns began to dip below the horizon and he knew that night would soon fall out here. He wouldn't slow for that either, but ride all night if he had to. Nothing would stop him.

Finally, up ahead, the commander spotted something in the distance, some break in the monotony of this flat landscape. They bore down on it, and as they did, he recognized what it was: a tree. A huge, twisted tree, by itself in the middle of nowhere.

He followed the trail until it ended, right beneath the tree. Of course it would end here, he thought: they would seek shade, shelter. He could use it himself.

He came to a stop beneath the tree and his men all followed, all of them gasping as they dismounted, beyond exhausted. He was, too, but he did not pay attention. Instead, he was too focused on the trail.

He looked down and studied it, baffled. The trail seemed to disappear into thin air. It did not proceed in any direction once they reached it.

"They must have died beneath the tree," said one of his men.

The commander frowned, annoyed by their stupidity.

"Then where are their bones?" he demanded.

"They must have been eaten," another added. "Bones and all. Look there!"

There came a rustling noise, and the commander followed his men's worried glance as they pointed to the tree branches, way up high, hiding scores of tree clingers. The beasts watched them carefully, as if debating whether to pounce.

His men hurried out from beneath the tree, but the Commander stayed put, unafraid. If they killed him, so be it—he was not concerned. He was more concerned with losing the tracks, with reporting back to Volusia as a failure.

"Let us go," said one of his men, laying a hand on his shoulder. "Night falls. I am sorry. Our search is over. We must return now. They died here, and that is what we must tell Volusia."

"And bring back no proof?" the commander asked. "Are you as stupid as you look? Do you now know that she would kill us?"

The commander ignored his men and instead stood there and looked out, peering into the desert, hands on hips. He listened for a long time, to the sound of the blowing wind, of the rustling branches, listening for all the signs, the faintest clues. He closed his eyes and smelled the dusty air, using all of his senses.

When he opened his eyes, he looked down and studied the ground, his nose telling him something—and this time, he spotted a tiny dot of red.

He knelt beside it and tasted the dirt.

"Blood," he reported. "Fresh blood." He looked up and studied the horizon, feeling a new certainty rise within him. "Someone died here recently."

He smiled as he stood and looked down and began to realize.

"Ingenious," he said.

"What, Commander?" one of his men asked.

"Someone tried to cover it up," he said. It was indeed ingenious, he realized, and he knew it would have fooled any other tracker—but not him.

"Gwendolyn is alive," he said. "She went that way—and she's not alone. There are new people with her. And I would bet anything, anything in the world, that she will lead us right into the lap of the Ridge."

The commander mounted his zerta and took off, not waiting for the others, following his instincts, which were leading him, he knew, toward a new horizon—and toward his ultimate glory.

CHAPTER THIRTY

Kendrick woke to a cool breeze on his face, his head on the hard desert floor, and knew immediately that something was wrong.

He sat up quickly and looked all around him, on alert. The warrior within had always told him when danger lurked, when something had imperceptibly shifted in the air. He saw Brandt and Atme, Koldo and Ludvig and all the others lying about the fire, now just embers, as the first of the two suns began to rise, lighting the sky a scarlet red. Everything was still, and at first glance everyone seemed to be here and all seemed to be well. He squinted into the horizon and saw no threat, no monsters of any kind.

Yet still, some sense within him told him something was not right. Kendrick wondered if it was just the nightmares he'd had, plaguing him all night as he tossed on the hard desert floor, swatting away bugs. Yet he knew better.

Kendrick slowly rose to his feet as the sun rose higher, the sky lightening just a bit, and as he surveyed the camp once again, suddenly he saw it: there, in the distance, were tracks, leading away from his camp. Footprints.

Kendrick looked back and itemized all the bodies lying about the fire and he suddenly realized, his heart skipping a beat, that one was missing:

Kaden.

There came a quiet clanging of armor, and Kendrick turned to see the men slowly, one by one, rising in the desert morning, all looking at him, standing there in wonder. They saw Kendrick looking cautiously out into the desert, and they lay their hands on the hilt of their swords, on guard, too.

Koldo came up beside him.

"There," Kendrick said.

Koldo followed his glance, down to the desert floor, and as he saw the footprints, his eyes widened. He immediately turned and scanned the camp.

"Kaden," Koldo said, alarm in his voice. "He is missing."

All the others rose to their feet and began to walk to the footprints, examining them, while Ludvig knelt down beside them, ran his finger in them, and looked up to the horizon.

"Kaden was the last on patrol last night," said a young soldier, who stood there, looking panicked. "I gave him the torch before I fell asleep. He was on dawn patrol. I remembered, he ventured out there by himself."

"Why?" Koldo demanded.

The soldier looked up, nervous, unsure.

"He said he wanted to go further. He wanted to prove to the others that he was unafraid."

Kendrick looked down at the footsteps, and it all suddenly made sense. This fine young man, going out there alone, wanting to prove himself after Naten made fun of him in front of the others. It made Kendrick hate Naten even more.

They all set out, as one, wordlessly following the trail, and after about twenty paces, Kendrick looked down and was surprised to see the trail changed dramatically. In place of one set of footprints, there were dozens of other prints. Unusually shaped creatures' prints. They trailed off into the horizon.

They all studied it with grave concern.

Ludvig knelt, examining the prints, rubbing the sand between his fingers. He then looked up and watched the trail lead off into the flat, merciless desert horizon, in the opposite direction of the sand wall.

"Sand Walkers," Ludvig announced grimly. "They've taken him."

A heavy silence fell over all of them as the reality of the situation sank in: Kaden, the King's youngest son, their crown jewel, had been abducted. The silence was so heavy and the tension so thick, Kendrick could cut it with a knife.

"Those tracks lead away from the Ridge," Naten stepped up and said, frowning accusingly at Kendrick, as if this were all his fault. "If we go after him, we will all die out there."

Koldo scowled at him.

"If you're so concerned with your life, turn back and head for the Ridge."

Koldo held his scowl until Naten looked away, shamed.

"In fact," Koldo said, raising his voice, "I want all of you to go back. What we don't need are all of us, on foot, heading out into the

Waste. We need horses. And speed, to catch them. All of you go back, carry back our dead, and return to me with horses."

"And you?" Naten asked. "You will travel alone, on foot, away from the Ridge, against a tribe of Sand Walkers? You will die."

Koldo stared back firmly.

"There is no shame in death," he replied. "Only in turning our backs on our brothers."

Kendrick felt his heart swell, and at that moment, he knew exactly what was the right thing to do.

"I shall go with you," Kendrick said.

"And I," said Brandt and Atme, and all the members of the Silver.

"And I, my brother," Ludvig said, laying a hand on Koldo's shoulder. "After all, he is my brother, too."

Kendrick could see the look of gratitude and mutual admiration in Koldo's eyes.

"Far be it from me to turn away someone else's valor," Koldo replied.

Kendrick, resigned, turned to his men.

"Brandt and Atme, you may join us," Kendrick said, "but the rest of you Silver, return with the men of the Ridge. If we should die, some Silver must live, to pass on our history to future generations. Return to us with horses."

The other Silver grudgingly nodded and backed down.

Kendrick watched as the men of the Ridge, along with the remaining Silver, turned and began walking quickly away, back in the direction of the Ridge. He turned and faced Koldo, Ludvig, Brandt, and Atme. Now there were but five of them, alone, out here in the Waste, and about to head even deeper into it.

They exchanged a look of honor, of fearlessness, of resignation, of mutual respect. Nothing more need be said: Kaden was out there somewhere, and all of them, each one of them, would risk their lives to get him back.

The five of them, together, turned fearlessly and marched out into the Waste, into the rising suns, one step at a time, on their ultimate quest of honor.

CHAPTER THIRTY ONE

Volusia sat on her terrace overlooking the coliseum, relieved to be back here, without distraction, after having killed Romulus's men, and to be able to immerse herself in the games. She was especially excited to watch this fight which, for the first time, kept her on the edge of her seat—it was the one they called "Darius" who fought. He was unlike any of the other gladiators, a brilliant fighter, one who actually survived. She admired his courage—but she admired bloodlust more, and looked forward to watching him getting carved to pieces.

"Goddess," came a voice.

Volusia spun, in a rage, to see several of her generals standing close by.

"The next person who interrupts me will be thrown into the ring," she snapped.

A general, nervous, terrified, exchanged a look with another.

"But Goddess, this is urgent—"

Volusia jumped from her seat and faced one of her generals, who stood there, fear across his face. All her other advisors grew quiet with fear as they watched.

"I'll make you a deal," she said. "If it is truly urgent, then I shall let you live. But if it is not, and you have interrupted my viewing pleasure for nothing, then I will kill you here and now."

She gripped his wrist, and he wiped sweat from his forehead, clearly debating. Finally, he spoke:

"It is urgent, Goddess."

She smiled.

"Very well, then," she replied. "It is your life to lose."

He gulped, then said, in a rush:

"I bear news from the streets of Volusia," he said. "There is a great outcry amongst your citizens. Everywhere, the Volks have spread out, killing and gorging on innocent people. They tear off their heads with their teeth, and suck on their blood. At first, it was just a few—but now they slaughter our people everywhere. They are torturing and killing our people and they have free rein in the streets. What's more," he continued, "word arrives from the east: the Knights of the Seven are close, and they bring with them an army greater than all the earth. They say they are seven million men—and they are all approaching the capital."

Volusia looked at him, her mind racing with a million thoughts, but mostly annoyance at being interrupted from the arena. She released her grip on his wrist, and he stood up straighter, clearly relieved.

"You spoke the truth," she said. "Your message *was* urgent. For that, I thank you."

Then in one swift motion, she drew her dagger and sliced his throat.

He stared back at her, wide-eyed in shock, as he collapsed to the ground, dead at her feet.

She smiled.

"That part about sparing you," she added. "I changed my mind."

Volusia felt her body grow hot with a flash of rage as she thought of the Volks, out there gorging on all her citizens. She had given them too much free rein.

"Enough is enough, Goddess," said Aksan, her trusted advisor and assassin. "The Volks have grown uncontrollable. You cannot control them. They will turn against you, too, eventually. They must be stopped, regardless of whatever powers they wield."

Volusia had been thinking the same thing.

She grudgingly rose from her seat and marched from her chamber, beginning to take the steps down toward the streets of Volusia.

The Volks, she knew, were the source of all the power she had. She needed them. Yet at the same time, they were an even greater threat to her.

She knew she had no choice. She could not have people around her she could not control—especially sorcerers whose power was greater than hers. Perhaps her advisors had been right all along when they'd advised her not to enter into a pact with the Volks; perhaps there was a reason they had been shunned throughout the Empire.

Volusia, followed by her entourage, marched down the streets of the capital, and as she went, she looked up and in the distance saw hundreds of citizens on their backs, the green Volks on top of them pinning them down, sucking the blood from their throats as their bodies writhed.

Everywhere she looked she saw Volks gorging themselves, slaughtering her people. And there, in the center, beneath a statue of her, was the leader of the Volks, Vokin, gorging on several bodies at once.

Volusia approached him, determined to put an end to this chaos, to expel him and his people. Her heart thumped as she wondered how he would react—she feared it would not be good. Yet she took comfort in the fact that she had all her generals behind her and that they would not dare touch her, a goddess.

Volusia came up to him and stood over him, and as she did, he finally stopped gorging and looked up at her, still snarling, his sharp fangs dripping with blood. He icily recognized Volusia, darkness in his eyes, looking mad to be interrupted.

"And what do you want, Goddess?" he asked, his voice throaty, nearly snarling.

Volusia was furious, not only by his actions, but by his lack of respect.

"I want you to leave," she commanded. "You will leave my service at once. I expel you from the capital. You will take your men and walk out the gates and never come back again."

Vokin slowly and menacingly stood and rose to his full height— which was not much—and breathing hard, raspy, he glared back at Volusia. As she watched his eyes shift colors, demonic, for the first time, she felt real fear.

"Will I?" he mocked.

He took a step toward her and as he did, all of the Volk suddenly rushed to his side—while all of her generals nervously drew their swords behind her.

A thick tension hung in the air as the two sides faced off with each other.

"Would you be so brazen as to confront a goddess?" Volusia demanded.

Vokin laughed.

"A goddess?" he echoed. "Whoever said you were one?"

She glared back at him, but she felt real fear rising within her as he took another step closer. She could smell his awful smell even from here.

"No one dismisses the Volks," he continued. "Not you, not anyone. For the dishonor you have inflicted upon us this day, for the injustice you have served, do you really think there will be no price to pay?"

Volusia stood proudly, feeling the goddess within her taking over. She knew, after all, that she was invincible.

"You will walk away," she said, "because my powers are greater than yours."

"Are they?" he replied.

He smiled wide, an awful look that she would recall for the rest of her life, burned into her mind, as he reached up with his long, slimy green fingers and stroked the side of her face.

"And yet, I fear," he said, "you are not as powerful as you think."

As he caressed her cheek, Volusia shrieked; she suddenly felt a searing pain course into her cheeks, run along her face, all over her skin. Wherever his fingers had touched, she felt as if her skin were melting away, burning off of her cheekbones.

Volusia sank to her knees and shrieked, feeling in more pain than she could conceive, shocked that she, a goddess, could ever feel such pain.

Vokin laughed as he reached down and held out a small golden looking glass for her to see herself in.

As Volusia looked at her own reflection, her pain worsened: she saw herself, and she wanted to throw up. While half of her face remained beautiful, the other half had become melted, distorted. Her appearance was the scariest thing she had ever seen, and she felt like dying at the sight of herself.

Vokin laughed, a horrific sound.

"Take a long look at yourself, Goddess," he said. "Once you were famed for your beauty—now you will be famed for being grotesque. Just like us. It is our goodbye present to you. After all, don't you know that the Volks cannot leave without giving a departing gift?"

He laughed and laughed as he turned and walked away, out the city gates, followed by his army of sorcerers, Volusia's source of power. And Volusia could do nothing but kneel there, clutching her face, and shrieking to the heavens with the cracking voice of a goddess.

CHAPTER THIRTY TWO

Gwendolyn ascended the spiral stone staircase in the far corner of the King's castle, her heart pounding with anticipation, as she headed for Argon's chamber. The King had graciously given Argon the grand chamber at the top of the spiral tower to recover, and had also vowed to Gwendolyn that he would give him his finest healers. Gwendolyn had been nervous to see him ever since; after all, the last time she had seen him, he was still comatose, and she was skeptical he would ever rise again.

Jasmine's words had encouraged her that Argon was healing, and her cryptic reference to what Argon knew about finding Thor and Guwayne was consuming her. Was there something he was holding back from her? Why would he not reveal it? And how did a young girl know all this?

Gwen, desperate for any chance, any lead, to be able to reunite with her husband and son, burned with desire as she reached the top floor and rushed up to the large arched door to his chamber.

Two of the King's guards stood before it, but when they saw the look on her face, they thought better of it.

"Open this door at once," she said, using the voice of a Queen.

They exchanged a look and stepped aside, opening the door as she rushed inside.

Gwendolyn entered the chamber, the door slamming behind her, and as she did, she was startled at the sight before her. There, in the magnificent spiral tower, was a beautiful chamber, shaped in a circle, its walls made of cobblestone, its walls lined with stained glass. Even more shocking was what she saw: Argon, sitting up in bed, awake, alert, looking right at her, wearing his white robes and holding his staff. She was elated to see him alive, conscious, back to his old self. She was even more surprised to see, sitting beside the bed, a woman, who looked ageless, with long silky hair parted in the middle, and wearing a green, silk gown. Her eyes glowed red, and she sat perfectly erect, with one hand on Argon's back, the other on his shoulder, and hummed softly, her eyes closed. Gwen realized at once that she must be the King's personal healer, the one responsible for Argon's recovery.

What's more, Gwen immediately sensed the connection between the two of them, sensed that they liked each other. It was strange—Gwen had never imagined Argon falling in love. But looking at the two of them, they seemed perfect together. Each a powerful sorcerer.

Gwen stopped in her tracks, so startled at the sight, she didn't know what to say.

Argon looked at her, and his eyes lit up with intensity as he stood to his full height, holding his staff. She sensed with relief that his great power had returned to him.

"You live," she said, astounded.

He nodded back and smiled ever so slightly.

"I do indeed," he replied. "Thanks to your carrying me through the desert. And to Celta's help."

Celta nodded back to Argon, their eyes locking.

Gwen wanted to rush forward and hug him, yet she was conflicted; she was mad at him for his not telling her whatever he knew that kept her from finding her husband and son.

"What do you know about Thor?" she demanded. "And Guwayne? And why did you not tell me you had a brother?"

Argon just looked back at her, eyes aglow, never wavering, lost in distant worlds she knew she would never understand. Some part of him was always unreachable, even to her.

"Not all knowledge is meant to be revealed," he finally replied.

Gwen frowned, refusing to accept no for an answer.

"Guwayne is my *son*," she said. "Thor is my husband. I deserve to know where they are. I *need* to know where they are," she said, stepping forward, desperate.

Argon gazed back at her for a long time, then finally sighed, turned, and walked to the window, looking out.

"Many centuries ago," he said to her, "before your father's father, and his father before him, my brother and I were close. Yet time has a way of forking even the strongest rivers, and over time, we grew apart. This universe was not big enough to hold two brothers—not brothers like Ragon and I."

Argon fell silent for a long time, gazing out the window.

"It became clear that Ragon's place was here, in the Ridge, on this side of the world," he continued, "while mine was elsewhere, in the Ring. We were two sides of the same coin, two faces of the same father—much like the two sides of the Ring and the Ridge."

As Argon fell silent again, Gwen processed it all. It was hard to imagine: Argon and Ragon's father. She was overflowing with questions, but she held her tongue.

Finally, he began again.

"My place was in the Ring, protecting the Canyon, holding up the Shield. Guarding the Destiny Sword, while Ragon guarded the Ridge. We lived this way for many, many centuries."

"But he's not here now," Gwen said, puzzled.

Argon shook his head.

"No, he is not."

"Where is he then?" she asked.

"Ragon foresaw the end of the Ridge," Argon replied, "and he took the steps needed to save it. He's in exile, on the Isle of Light, preparing for the second coming."

"Second coming?" Gwen asked.

Argon sighed long and hard, staying silent. Gwen did not want to pry, but she needed to know where this was all going, and how it related to Thor.

"What I want to know is about Thorgrin and Guwayne," she finally insisted. "What are you not telling me?"

Argon looked anguished as he looked at the window, until finally, he turned and looked at her. The intensity of his gaze was overwhelming.

"Some things are given to us in life," he said gravely, "while others are taken away. We must celebrate what we have while we have it. And when something is lost to us, we must allow it to leave."

Gwen felt her heart sinking at his words.

"What are you saying?" she demanded.

He took two steps toward her, standing a few feet away, staring back with such intensity that she had to look away. She had never seen him wear such a serious expression.

"Your husband is gone," he pronounced gravely, each of his words like a blow to her heart. "Your son is gone to you, too. I am sorry, but they will never return. Not as you know them."

Gwen felt like collapsing.

"NO!" she shrieked, crying, everything bursting out of her. She ran forward and grabbed Argon's robe, and beat him on his chest with her fists, again and again.

Argon stood there, expressionless, not fighting her off but not comforting her either.

"I am sorry," he said, after several moments. "I loved Thorgrin as a son. And Guwayne, too."

"NO!" she shrieked, refusing to accept it.

Gwen turned and ran out the chamber, down the corridor, and burst out onto the wide parapets atop the castle. She stood there, all alone, clutching the rail and searching the horizon. She looked out at the distant peaks, the mist hanging over the ridge. Somewhere beyond was the Great Waste, and beyond that, the great sea. Carrying Thorgrin and Guwayne.

She could not accept her fate. Never.

"NO!" Gwen shrieked to the heavens. "Come back to me!"

CHAPTER THIRTY THREE

Thor felt a deepening sense of foreboding as he gripped the rail, standing at the bow of the ship, and stared out at the Straits of Madness, looming before him. Red waters of blood churned below as they carried the ship on their currents, into the straits. Thor looked side to side, staring up in awe, as did the others, at the stark black cliffs, jagged, rising straight up, made of a black stone he did not recognize. They were close together, leaving but twenty yards of angry waters for them to pass through, and Thor felt claustrophobic, the sky nearly shut out. He also felt vulnerable to attack, especially as he examined the cliffs and spotted thousands of sets of small, yellow eyes, glowing, peeking out from tiny holes in the rocks, then disappearing. He felt as if they were being watched by a million creatures.

But that was not what concerned him most. As they entered the Straits, the water churned violently, rocking their ship side to side, up and down—and Thor began to hear something, rising over the din of the waves and the wind. It was soft at first, like a distant humming; as they went, though, it grew stronger. It was almost like a chanting, like a chorus of voices humming in a low pitch. It sounded like a drumbeat, felt like his heart was beating outside his head; it echoed inside his innermost eardrum, and the feeling was making him go mad.

Thor clutched the rail, experiencing a feeling he'd never felt before; it was almost like an unwelcome invader entering his body. He felt, for the first time in his life, that he was losing control of himself. As if he could no longer think straight.

The chanting grew louder, and as it did, he felt increasingly on edge; every little sound was amplified inside him: the splashing of the water against the hull; the flapping of the sails; the sound of those insects, buzzing; the screech of a bird high overhead. He could not turn it off, and it was driving him crazy.

Thor began to feel a rage rising in his veins, one he could not control or understand. It was consuming him, making him want to lash out, to kill something—anything. He didn't understand where it was coming from, and as they sailed still deeper into the Straits, he felt it taking over him completely. As if it owned his very soul.

Thor gripped the rail so hard his knuckles turned white as he tried to control himself, to exorcise himself of whatever was consuming him. He looked out at the others, hoping they would see the horror he was going through and would be rushing to help him.

But as Thor saw the others, his apprehension only deepened. He could see at a glance that whatever madness had gripped him had gripped the others, too. There was Elden, rushing forward and head-butting the mast, again and again; there was Angel, curled up in a ball on the floor, holding her head; there was Selese, rocking left and right, her arms wrapped around herself; Matus knelt on the deck, pulling his hair from his head; Reece drew his sword then sheathed it, again and again; O'Connor paced the decks wildly, racing up and down them, as if trying to get off the boat; and Indra raised her spear and hurled it into the deck, only to remove it and do it again and again.

Thor realized that they'd all gone mad. For the first time in his life he could not think clearly, could not come up with a strategy to sail out of here, to rescue everyone, to burst free. He could not think at all. He just felt like he was becoming a ball of rage, growing bigger and bigger, one he could not control, even with his greatest powers. A titanic struggle was going on inside him.

And he was losing.

Thor screamed as he sank to his knees, feeling like tearing off his own skin, his head splitting, the chanting growing louder and louder inside his head as the boat rocked more violently. Thor felt as if he had to kill something—anything—to make it stop.

Thor looked down and saw himself gripping the hilt of the Sword of the Dead, squeezing it and letting it go, squeezing and letting go, his hand almost moving on its own accord. As he examined it, he saw the small faces on the hilt begin to move, frowning, as if the sword itself were coming alive. The sword, too, Thor realized, was being affected by these straits of madness.

Thor found himself drawing the sword from its sheath, against his will; he tried to put it back with all his might, but he was unable to. The Sword gripped him, and the madness was commanding him. Thor was burning to kill whatever foe he could, to make it all stop.

But the problem was, there was no foe. There was nothing but air.

Thor heard a shout, and as he turned, he could not believe what he saw: there went O'Connor, running across the ship, screaming— and then, jumping up onto the rail and leaping off one side, diving through the air.

"O'CONNOR!" Thor shouted.

But it was too late. There was nothing Thor could do but watch, helplessly, as O'Connor dove over the edge, head-first, plunging a good thirty feet toward the red raging waters below. O'Connor reached up and flailed before being immediately swept away by them—then sucked down beneath the surface.

No one came to his help—all of them, including Thor, too preoccupied with their own private hells. Soon, O'Connor's screams stopped, and Thor felt an unspeakable agony as he knew they had just lost a Legion member forever.

Thor was burning to jump in and save him, but he could not. And as he tried with all his might to re-sheath his sword, he could not do that, either. His hands shook with the effort—but it was stronger than he.

Suddenly, to Thor's horror, he realized he was aiming the tip of the sword at himself, at his own heart. His hands shook as he realized he was going to kill himself.

Thor sensed motion and looked up to see Reece walking toward him, battling himself, sheathing and unsheathing his sword, a pained, confused look on his face. For a moment Reece seemed to get a hold of himself, to become stronger than whatever it was.

"Be strong, Thorgrin!" Reece shouted out, above the din of the wind and the raging sea. "We can fight this. We are stronger than this!"

Thor tried to hear his friend's words, but the chanting within him grew too loud, the drumbeat of rage, egging him on.

"We are almost there, Thorgrin!" Reece shouted. "Just a few more feet!"

Thor followed his gaze and turned to see the end of the Straits of Madness looming, the cliffs parting ways, the waters calming, the sky breaking into light.

But even though it was just a few feet away, it was too far for him. It might as well have been on the other end of the world.

Thor could not stand it another second. He could no longer contain the rage, the desire to kill.

In one horrifying moment, a moment that would haunt Thorgrin for the rest of his life, he found himself standing and, with shaking hands, redirecting the tip of the sword away from his own chest. Instead, he was horrified to see, he was turning it—and directing it at Reece.

Reece looked down and watched, and his face fell in horror as he, too, realized what Thor was about to do.

But neither of them could control it, both in the grips of something far more powerful than they.

Thor, helpless to do otherwise, found himself stepping forward, raising his sword, and as Reece reached out to console him, plunging it right into the beating heart of his best friend in the world.

Thor could do nothing but stand there and gasp as he held Reece tight, and killed the man he loved most in the world.

CHAPTER THIRTY FOUR

Darius lay on his back and looked up and watched one of those creatures raise its ax high overhead and bring it down right for his face. His world moved in slow motion: he felt every breeze, saw the frozen face of the beast, heard the distant cheers of the crowd. This was what it felt like, he realized, to live his last breath.

Darius wanted to react in time, to roll out of the way or block the blow—yet he knew he could not. His sword lay two feet away, and this time the creature had come down too fast for him to react in time. Out of the corner of his eye Darius saw his fellow gladiators, all dead on the ground, and he knew that his time, too, had come. Here he would meet his end, on this dusty floor, in this hated arena, with all these gladiators whom he did not know, killed by this horrific beast.

Darius had no regrets. He had fought proudly, had not backed down, and had faced whatever they had thrown at him. At least he would have a chance now to reunite with his brothers in arms—Raj, Desmond, Kaz, and Luzi—and join them in the world to come. Darius thought of Loti, and he wondered if she, too, were dead, waiting to greet him, or is she was still alive somewhere. He did not know which was worse.

The blade came closer, and Darius felt its breeze and prepared to die—when suddenly, a clang rang in his ears. Darius blinked and looked up to see the giant ax blade stopped by a long, silver staff, just inches above his face.

Darius looked over and was shocked to see Deklan, standing there calmly in his brown robes, staring back defiantly at the beast as he held out his silver staff, blocking its blow and saving Darius's life.

Darius blinked several times, not understanding what he was seeing. What was Deklan doing here? Why had he risked his life for him? How could he be so strong as to block such a terrific blow with his silver staff?

As Darius stared in disbelief, still trying to process it all, trying to process that he was still alive, he watched Deklan break into action. Deklan spun his staff in a circle, throwing the ax from the creature's hand, then pulled back his staff and jabbed the creature between the eyes, knocking it backwards.

The great ax spun in the air, and Deklan reached out and snatched it seamlessly, then as several creatures charged him, he pulled it back and threw it. It sailed end over end through the air then lodged itself in a creature's head—to the delight of the crowd—felling it.

In the same motion Deklan swung his staff around and smashed another creature on the side of the head, making it drop its ax in mid-blow and sending it to its knees. Other creatures descended upon him, but Deklan faced them all calmly, hardly even looking distressed as he sidestepped them and swung his staff in every direction, end over end, striking one here and another there, moving like lightning as he darted between them. He was constantly in motion, like a cat, moving with stunning speed and dexterity; he was more agile and graceful than any fighter Darius had ever seen.

Deklan spun and jabbed one in the wrist, disarming him, then broadsided one in the throat, then dodged and swept out another from behind his knees, then rolled and swung upward, hitting another between the legs. He created a circle of devastation around him, blocking or dodging their blows, moving so quickly that no one could touch him. He was like a whirlwind, and he did not stop until all the creatures lay on the ground before him.

With a pause in the battle, Deklan walked over to Darius, calm and cool, and reached out a hand.

Darius looked up, shocked, still hardly believing what had happened. He took Deklan's hand and he yanked him to his feet.

Deklan smiled back.

"Figured I couldn't let you have all the fun," he said with a grin.

Deklan picked up a dropped ax, stepped forward, and slashed Darius's chains, freeing him.

The crowd roared in surprise and delight, and Darius turned and took it all in, standing there with Deklan in the eye of the tornado, seeing all the felled creatures, all about to rise again. He stared back at Deklan in awe, wondering. He had never encountered a greater warrior. Who was this man?

All around them, the creatures were slowly rising, and as Darius tightened his grip on an ax handle, he felt emboldened. Standing side by side with Deklan, he felt that, for the first time, he could win.

"I don't understand," Darius said, as they waited, back to back, for the creatures to come again. "Why did you risk your life for me?"

"I realized you were right," he said. "Life is a small thing. Honor matters more. Somewhere along the path, I lost my way. You helped me find it again. I am done surviving: now I choose to live—and to live with honor."

"But why me?" Darius insisted, something bothering him. "Why give it all up, why risk your life for *me*, a stranger?"

There came a pause, amidst the roar of the crowd, as more creatures gained their feet, assembling like a small army to come back for them. Darius braced himself, as he knew the fight of his life was coming.

"Because, Darius," Deklan finally replied, "you are no stranger."

Darius looked back at him, puzzled, and as he did, he finally recognized something in the man's eyes, something that had been at the edge of his consciousness, something that finally had it all make sense.

"Because you, Darius," he said, bracing himself for the coming blows, "are my son."

COMING SOON!

BOOK #17 IN THE SORCERER'S RING

Books by Morgan Rice

THE SORCERER'S RING
A QUEST OF HEROES
A MARCH OF KINGS
A FATE OF DRAGONS
A CRY OF HONOR
A VOW OF GLORY
A CHARGE OF VALOR
A RITE OF SWORDS
A GRANT OF ARMS
A SKY OF SPELLS
A SEA OF SHIELDS
A REIGN OF STEEL
A LAND OF FIRE
A RULE OF QUEENS
AN OATH OF BROTHERS
A DREAM OF MORTALS

THE SURVIVAL TRILOGY
ARENA ONE (Book #1)
ARENA TWO (Book #2)

the Vampire Journals
turned (book #1)
loved (book #2)
betrayed (book #3)
destined (book #4)
desired (book #5)
betrothed (book #6)
vowed (book #7)
found (book #8)
resurrected (book #9)
craved (book #10)
fated (book #11)

About Morgan Rice

Morgan Rice is the #1 bestselling author of THE VAMPIRE JOURNALS, a young adult series comprising eleven books (and counting); the #1 bestselling series THE SURVIVAL TRILOGY, a post-apocalyptic thriller comprising two books (and counting); and the #1 bestselling epic fantasy series THE SORCERER'S RING, comprising fifteen books (and counting).

Morgan's books are available in audio and print editions, and translations of the books are available in German, French, Italian, Spanish, Portugese, Japanese, Chinese, Swedish, Dutch, Turkish, Hungarian, Czech and Slovak (with more languages forthcoming).

Morgan loves to hear from you, so please feel free to visit www.morganricebooks.com to join the email list, receive a free book, receive free giveaways, download the free app, get the latest exclusive news, connect on Facebook and Twitter, and stay in touch!

9 781632 911315